12
Parables

12 Parables

Wayne Faust

Healthy Life Press
Orlando, Florida

12 Parables

Library of Congress Cataloging-in-Publication Data
Faust, Wayne
    12 Parables (Revision 1)

ISBN 978-1-939267-06-1

1. Fiction; 2. Christian Fiction; 3. Classic & Allegory

Information about the author's touring schedule and a selection of his music are available at his website: www.waynefaust.com.

Dedication

To
Eleanor Faust
1927-1989
Thanks, Mom

Wayne Faust

Acknowledgements

First of all, I'd like to thank Dave Biebel at Healthy Life Press for believing in this project, and enduring all the really fun tasks like deciding which words to capitalize and which to leave in lower case. It's been a real joy working with you.

Thanks to Dave's wife, Ilona, for reading these stories and providing helpful encouragement throughout the process.

Thanks to my wife, Sally, for letting me read most of these stories out loud to her, so I could see how the text flowed and see if I was actually getting my point across. Through thirty-five years of marriage, she's played this valuable role for me, both with my songs and with my prose.

Thanks to Pamela Tyree Griffin at Joyful online magazine (www.joyfulonline.net), where some of these stories were first published. It was her comment, "You should put these in a book someday!" that started me down this road.

Thanks to all the pastors out there, laboring to write sermons every Sunday so all of us can be edified. Many of the ideas for these stories came from when I was in church or online, listening to sermons.

And finally, thanks to my Lord for not giving up on me when I was trying so desperately to run away from Him. I hope this project shines just a little light on His glorious face.

Wayne Faust
March 2011

Preface

Parables, parables. Where do they come from?

It's a very old way of telling a tale. Jesus Himself was a master storyteller, using Parables freely to make an important point in an entertaining way. I've always loved reading biblical parables and discussing what they might mean. So when I first became a Christian and I started listening to sermons and reading books about spiritual issues, my brain immediately began to think in terms of, "How can I say this in a different way? How can I write a story about this?"

I've been writing songs all my life, especially funny songs, where you have to make your point in three verses or less. So when I started writing stories, most of them ended up being short, compact, and tightly written. When I started writing stories about Christian spiritual things, they too were very short and compact, the kind of stories you could present aloud at church. It was then that I said to myself, "Wow! I'm writing parables!"

I sent off a couple to Pamela Tyree Griffin at Joyful Online (joyfulonline.net) and, lo and behold, she published them. Pretty soon, I had five stories with Joyful and more stories kept coming to me, especially while I was in church. For instance, during communion one Sunday, I was thinking of how wonderful it would be if the whole world could be having this simple meal together, all at the same time. I went home and wrote "The Meal" in one sitting. And on and on.

Last fall, I was cutting firewood at my friend Monte Swan's land in the foothills of Colorado. Monte and his friend, Dave Biebel, had published a book called, *Romancing Your Child's Heart*, before Dave established Healthy Life Press. Dave was visiting Monte, and that's where I met him. After I went home with my firewood secured for the winter, I got to thinking, "Hey, that guy's a Christian publisher. And I do have these parables. . . ."

Well, one thing led to another and now here we are with "12 Parables." It was a real joy to write this book, and it was so much fun to see how the story ideas just kept on coming, especially when I was up against a deadline. I hope it was the Lord working through me when that happened. Ever since finishing the stories in this book, the ideas keep on coming. So hopefully, this will not be the last book of parables I will write.

Maybe someday they'll call me a Parablist. Is that a word?

Wayne Faust
March 2011

CONTENTS

PARABLE 1:
THE WALL

The world was aching. There was an emptiness in people's hearts and no one could remember a time when it hadn't been so. According to the scribes, the Tasks had been invented over five hundred years ago, but as much as they had tried, no one had ever done them all. Because of that, the Gate remained closed.

The Gate stood on top of a hill at the edge of the Capital. It reached up nearly to the clouds and it was set into an equally high Wall, which stretched all the way around the world.

No one had ever been to the top of the Wall, although on certain clear nights, you could see a warm, amber light glowing above it. It was this glow that caused such a longing in the people, for somehow they knew that God dwelled on the other side. But He was hopelessly out of reach.

****

"Father?" asked the young girl. "Did you ever try to open the Gate?"'

They had finished their prayers and the father was getting ready to blow out the candle.

"Many times," he said. "I once got to the twenty-seventh Task, but then I made a mistake and had to start all over. I never got that far again."

"How many Tasks are there?" asked the girl.

"No one knows. The best anyone has ever done is to get to number one hundred twenty-eight and that took over seven hours."

"Why can't the priests memorize the Tasks so they can keep going further until they make it to the end?"

The father smiled at the sharp intelligence of his daughter. "It would be wonderful if they could do that," he answered. "But the Tasks are different each time. And so far everyone has fallen short. So the Gate remains closed."

"Why do they keep trying?" asked the girl.

"Because to not try is to give up hope. And living without hope would be just too sad. You're very young and already you know that. Remember how sad you were when your mother died?"

The girl nodded.

"Things like that happen every day, to everybody. The Holy Writings tell us that if we can make ourselves worthy enough to get through the Gate, then we will be with God and He will wipe away every tear."

As if in answer to her father's words, the girl began to cry. "But what if the Gate never opens at all?" she asked.

The father gathered up the girl in his arms and rocked her softly. "The priests tell us that someday a Hero will come. He will be able to achieve every Task and then the Gate will open."

The little girl looked up. "When will this Hero come?"

"No one knows. But if we pray very hard, maybe we can make him come sooner."

"Then I'll pray all night long!" said the girl. And indeed she tried, but like most little girls, she fell asleep before the moon was high.

****

The excitement began a week later. The whole Capital was talking about the Stranger who had come to town and climbed the hill. He still hadn't come back down. Someone went up to see what he was doing and found him going through the Tasks like no other. There were whispers that maybe this could be the One, the long expected Hero.

The father and daughter made their way up the hill. They found hundreds of people near the Gate. The father, being very tall, was able to see over the crowd and he lifted his daughter onto his shoulders.

They saw the Stranger in front of the Wall. He wasn't much to look at and he had a thin voice that didn't command much power. But he was meeting each challenge from the Wall. Each time he finished one Task, writing would appear in the marble of the Gate instructing him on what to do next. The father remembered his own tries with the Tasks and felt guilty all over again at his failure. But the Stranger wasn't failing.

"How long has he been here?" asked the father to a woman standing beside him.

"Three days," she answered, and the father felt his heart race. *Is this unassuming Stranger the one?* he wondered.

"He looks very tired," said the daughter from her perch on her father's shoulders. And indeed, the Stranger looked exhausted. He was doing some kind of purification Task with a thorn bush. His hands were bleeding.

Three days, thought the father. *This is so much longer than anyone has ever gone and still the Gate remains closed. How much more can there be?*

As dusk came on it began to rain. The people turned away and headed down the hill into town, hoping against hope that the Stranger would somehow be able to finish all the Tasks.

****

Morning broke clear and bright. The father and daughter ascended the hill along with many others to check on the Stranger. They found him still at his work, although clearly at the end of his strength. He could barely lift his feet off the ground, but still he gathered plants for purification, and he recited verses from the Scriptures.

Occasionally he would stumble and fall, but he always

pushed himself to his feet again, however slowly. His hands and feet were both dripping blood, leaving small red spots in the dirt. The people wanted to give him strength, to cheer him on, but they were afraid to even whisper because that might break his concentration. They kept a close eye on the Gate, however, hoping that at any moment it would creak open.

The Stranger recited one more Holy verse in a weak, raspy voice. The words on the wall changed again. Three words appeared in very large letters, large enough for the whole crowd to read.

THE FINAL TASK

A gasp rose from the crowd. The three words faded. They were replaced by just one word, in letters stretching up and out of sight. It was three letters long, and blood red.

Someone began to cry.
Someone else said it must be a mistake.
The Stranger staggered. He put his hands on his hips and straightened up. He turned toward the crowd. Clearly, he was clearly having trouble breathing. He raised his arms and blood dripped from his hands. He took a deep breath, and with one last, shuddering effort, he managed to shout out two final words in a raspy voice.

"For you," he said.

Then the Stranger collapsed to the ground and was still.

****

No one moved for what seemed like forever. Then, a doctor pushed his way through the crowd and bent over the Stranger. He took the man's pulse. He looked up and shook his head.

"It said it was the Final Task," someone cried.

"Did he accomplish it?" someone else asked.

Everyone looked toward the Gate. The awful, blood red word had faded. But the Gate had not opened. Someone ran up and pushed on it, but it held fast. A woman pounded her fist on the marble, tears rolling down her cheeks. But it was no use.

"All for nothing," someone said. "The Gates were never meant to open at all."

As night fell, the people made their hopeless way down the long, long hill, and finally fell asleep in a world of mourning.

****

Three days later the daughter woke early. The city was quiet and still in shock. Even though she wasn't supposed to go outside on her own, the girl slipped from her house and made her way up the hill. Something drew her on. As the sun rose behind her, she approached the massive Wall.

The girl's eyes grew wide, for there was a gap in the Wall

where the Gate used to be. Soft amber light shone through from the other side. The girl could feel a warmth and an indescribable love come over her. Standing near the opening was the Stranger, smiling as bright as the sun. He was no longer disheveled, no longer beaten down.

AND HE WAS NO LONGER DEAD.

The girl was so stunned that she did the only thing she could think of. She ran back down the hill as fast as she could and woke her father.

Ten minutes later the father and daughter approached the Wall. The father saw the Stranger, now alive again, and he fell to his knees. He, too, felt the warmth and love radiating from the other side of the Wall. He felt a touch on his shoulder.

"Stand and enter," said the Stranger, who had approached the father and was now standing in front of him.

The father got to his feet, shaking. "But the Tasks," he sputtered. "How can I do what you did?"

The Stranger put both hands on the man's shoulders, and looked him straight in the eyes. "The Tasks are finished," he said. "I've done them all. For all time. For you."

The father wiped at his eyes. "What must I do then?"

"Enter. Simply enter," came the reply.

It was almost too much to believe. After a lifetime of failure, the father was being asked to simply walk forward. With a feeling of unspeakable joy, he took his daughter's hand and they both did just that, moving into the incredible Light on the other side of the Wall.

Parable 2:
The Cross

I had been running away my whole life. The Lord had been working on my heart, but I kept on running. I thought I could handle anything that came my way. I had learned to rely on myself because it had always worked. But then one day it did not work any more. Problems came into my life that I just couldn't fix, no matter how hard I tried. And the fact that I couldn't fix them shook me to the very core of my being. For the first time in my life, I felt truly lost. The rock I had been leaning on turned out to be made of sand.

I found myself wandering through the city at night, the way someone in the old days might have wandered in the wilderness. Yes, there were people everywhere, and buildings full of light. But it all seemed dark to me.

One night I was doing my usual rounds, hands in my pockets, head down, trudging along the city street. I came around a corner and for some reason I stopped and looked up. I found myself standing in front of a small city church, sandwiched between large buildings on either side. It didn't look like it belonged there. Cracked concrete steps led up to a single wooden door, nothing like the grand entryways of most city cathedrals. This was more like a chapel. But it was quaint and somehow appealing to me. Something told me to walk up those steps. So I did.

The door was unlocked and I stepped cautiously through. I found my way in the darkness to the front pew, smelling old varnish and candle wax. I looked up at the altar. A beam of moonlight shone through the window, il-luminating a simple wooden cross hanging on the wall.

The cross had no gold, no silver. It had no sculpture of Jesus hanging from it. But somehow, it seemed so beautiful to me, maybe the most beautiful thing I had ever seen. A message called to me from that wooden cross. It was the message I had been running away from for so long. It said that Jesus had died on a plain cross like this one. And He had done it for me. My life had meaning beyond myself. I could be saved - not through anything I might do or say or be, but because He had died for me, and that gave my life meaning and value beyond my ability to comprehend.

I had heard that message a thousand times before of course. But on this night it was like a beacon of light in the shadows of that church. It was as if the cross itself was speaking to me. I felt a burden lift from my heart. Tears filled my eyes and I knelt down and wept. At that moment I accepted the Lord and was saved. Saved forever.

I spent a long time in that pew, gazing up at that cross. I felt my heart change inside my chest and I left that church a new creation.

The next few weeks were wonderful. I made a new start in so many ways. The darkness that had been plaguing me was gone. I felt like I could reach out to the world for the first time in a long while. In my joy, I found myself wandering back to that little chapel in the evenings. I loved to sit in the front pew and look up at that simple cross, just like I had that first night.

One evening I was joined in the pew by a middle-aged man. He prayed a little and then turned to me.

"You've just been saved, haven't you?" he asked, warmly.

"Yes," I replied. "Is it that obvious?"

He chuckled. Then he gave me a hug. "Welcome to the Kingdom," he said.

"Thanks," I replied. I felt warm, knowing I was part of such a fellowship of believers.

"Where do you go to church?" he asked.

"No place right now," I said. "A friend invited me to his church Sunday morning. I think I'll go there."

The man frowned. "Let me show you something," he said. He brought out his Bible and began to read me verses, lots of verses. Then he produced a pamphlet that talked about the Sabbath. There seemed to be some question about whether the Sabbath was really on Sunday, or whether it was actually supposed to be on Saturday, just like in the Old Testament.

"You see," he said, "God intended us to worship on Saturday. The sign of real Christians is that they worship on God's Sabbath, not one made by men for convenience. Your friend's church is probably well-intentioned but they are in error. Look it up for yourself."

He handed me the pamphlet. "Take this and study it. The address to my church is on the back. We'd love to see you there this Saturday. In the meantime, I'll leave something here for you to remind you of what is important."

He pulled something out of his coat pocket. It was a banner that declared in big, blue letters, "SATURDAY SAB-BATH." He reached into another pocket and produced some tacks and a small hammer. He walked up to the cross and tacked the banner on one of the crossbeams.

"See, that's better," he said. "Now when you gaze up here you can know the truth."

After the man left I pocketed the pamphlet and again gazed up at the cross. The banner hung a little crookedly, covering some of the wood. But the cross was still beautiful.

The following week was hectic as usual and I found the need to return to the little church. Coming to that simple cross could calm me down, no matter what. I sat in the front pew and looked up. The man's banner was still there. As I was praying, a woman strolled by the altar, carrying some flowers. She stopped in front of me.

"New believer, huh?"

I nodded my head.

"Welcome to the Lord's house," she said. Her voice had a pleasant lilt.

"Thank you," I answered.

She sat down next to me. "Let me say a prayer for you."

The woman proceeded to pray and I prayed with her, feeling the warm presence of God's love. I finished and gazed up at the cross. She continued to pray. After a while she switched to a language I didn't recognize. She did this for awhile and then let out a sigh. A tear formed at the corner of her eye.

"What was that language you were speaking?" I asked.

She smiled. "I was speaking in tongues," she said. "Have you spoken in tongues yet?"

"I don't think so," I answered.

"Oh, but you must. That is the sign of a real Christian. It's God's language, a most wonderful thing."

She explained how she was able to speak in tongues and how I might achieve the same thing.

"I tell you what," she said encouragingly. "You work on it. If your faith is strong, you'll be able to do it. In the meantime, I'll leave something here to remind you."

She produced a banner. It simply said "TONGUES" in big, red letters. She walked up to the cross and tacked it up on the crossbeam opposite the other banner. She waved to me and left.

I tried to make my tongue form words it hadn't formed before. Nothing happened. I tried some more. Still nothing. Finally I went back to looking at my cross, feeling a little bit frustrated. The shape of the cross was becoming obscured by the banners. But I knew there was simple wood underneath, so I calmed down.

Two weeks later I was back. The banners were still up there on the cross, but I guessed it was good that I should be reminded of important things. I prayed for a while.

A man in a nice business suit sat down in the pew behind me. "Just recently sanctified?" he asked.

I wasn't sure what that meant but I nodded my head anyway.

"Praise the Lord," he said.

"Praise the Lord," I answered.

He came up and sat beside me. He asked me for my testimony. I told him a few things about my life, how I had been running away from the Lord for so long. I told him about a night in a bar when a stranger had witnessed to me, and how his words had stayed with me, even though I hadn't really wanted to hear them. And I told him how those words had helped me make my decision a few weeks ago, here in this little chapel. I said that I wished I knew the stranger's name because I would love to thank him now.

"That's awesome," said the man in the suit. He put his hand on my shoulder. "That fella did a wonderful thing. He risked his soul for you by going into such an evil place."

"Evil place?"

"Of course. The bar. Christians have no business in a bar. They must abstain from alcohol altogether." He produced a Bible and read me some verses.

"Well, now that you're saved," he said, "I'm sure this won't be a problem for you any more. The Spirit has set you free from all of that. But just in case, I'll leave you a reminder on this cross here."

He produced a sign that said "NO ALCOHOL" in bold, orange letters, and tacked it up to the center beam of the cross. "There," he said. "That's better." He smiled and walked away.

I went back to gazing at the cross but it didn't calm me as much as it had in the past. I figured I must be just tired so I stood up and turned to leave. I glanced at the cross one more time over my shoulder as I walked down the aisle toward the front door. I shook my head and left.

In the next weeks I went back less and less. Each time I went, someone would come along and tack up another banner. Pretty soon there were banners of all types draping the cross, overlapping each other and shouting their words until I couldn't hear anything else.

One banner said, "NO AMPLIFIED MUSIC."

Another said, "SUITS AND TIES ONLY."

Yet another said, "APPROVED LITURGY A MUST."

And on and on.

I stopped going to the church altogether. My life settled into a routine, so I didn't feel the need to go there anyhow. I could get by just fine. I was saved, after all.

I began to feel sad most of the time. Pressures built inside of me. Where was the peace I had found on that first night in the chapel? I had to know.

Finally, late one night, I could no longer resist the need to go to that little church. I had to come to the cross.

I walked down the aisle and saw that all the banners were still there, tacked to the cross. I sat down in the front pew. Well, I told myself, I guess all those rules are important, and if I study them long enough, I can become a good Christian, just like all those people who put the signs up in the first place.

I stared at the banners. I said their words aloud, over and over. My mind was muddled, as muddled as all those pieces of paper hanging there. Finally, in frustration, I closed my eyes and began to pray.

I must have prayed for an hour that night. As I prayed, a picture formed in my head. It was a picture of a cross - a simple, wooden cross, with an even simpler message. I remembered how that message had sounded to me, the first night I had seen my cross, in this very church.

I opened my eyes. The banners fluttered in a soft breeze and the sound was loud in the quiet little church. I stood up on shaky legs.

Slowly, I walked up to the altar. I reached out my hand and then pulled it back, like from a hot stove. Then I reached out again and touched one of the banners. I don't remember now which one it was. I grabbed a piece of it and pulled, tearing the paper. I saw wood underneath - beautiful, simple wood. I touched the cross and it felt rough and solid beneath my fingers.

I grabbed a larger piece of paper in my fist and pulled as hard as I could. There was a loud ripping sound as the whole banner came away in my hand. I crumbled it up and tossed it aside. I grabbed another banner and tore it to shreds. Pretty soon I was ripping and tearing like a madman, until there were no banners left. Crumpled paper was scattered all over the floor like snow. I gathered it all up in a big ball and threw it down the aisle as hard as I could.

I turned back to the cross. Moonlight beamed through the window, illuminating the unadorned wood. It was again the most beautiful thing I had ever seen. I touched the cross gently and fell to my knees. Tears filled my eyes.

"Thank you, Lord," I whispered. "Please help everyone who comes to this place see the cross this way - simple and so very beautiful."

I stayed on my knees that night for a very long time.

PARABLE 3:
THE MEAL

He was a young Boy and he lived in the big city, but it wasn't like you might think. Yes, the houses were so close together that if you put your arm out a window you could touch your neighbor's house. Everybody had tiny, postage stamp lawns. But the neighborhood was full of tall, majestic elm trees that lined the block, making a leafy green canopy over the street. And it was safe here, so safe that you could take a walk late at night without worrying. And best of all, there was a park on each end of the block, one with trees for climbing and the other with open fields for playing baseball and rolling down grassy hills.

It was a good place to grow up, which the Boy was in

the process of doing. He hadn't grown up all the way of course, for he was still a Boy. But he was old enough to ask the big questions. And on an afternoon in late summer when the shadows were growing long, he climbed a tall maple tree. It was one of his favorite things to do. And as he perched up on the highest branch he dared sit on, he asked the biggest question of all.

"Are you up there?" he whispered to the sky, hazy blue and dotted with wispy clouds.

There was no answer.

But the Boy didn't mind. He was enjoying one of the last, long days of summer before school started up again.

Being up here like this always made his heart swell. He took joy in every little thing – the warm breeze, the rich smell of green grass, the sturdy branch beneath him holding him up like the hand of a giant. Gazing out from his perch, he could see the tops of houses in the distance and the steeple of the church. Children ran through the park below, looking like tiny ants. Maybe that's why he was thinking about God. Was this what the world looked like to God as He gazed down from heaven?

As always, the Boy was content to just sit up here and let the day go by, both arms wrapped around a branch for support. And, as usual, his mind was full of wonder.

"I know you're up there," he said to the sky.

This time he heard a voice in response.

"Are you hungry?"

The voice had come from the ground far below.

Startled, the Boy nearly lost his grip. Swaying a few times, he steadied himself and looked down through the branches. A man was sitting on the park bench below, looking up.

"Are you hungry?" shouted the man again.

"Huh?" muttered the Boy.

"I've got some dinner," said the man.

Even though the man was far below, the Boy could see him well enough. His smile seemed warm and inviting. The Boy suddenly noticed that he was, indeed, very hungry. His stomach rumbled a few times.

"Come on down," said the man. "There's more than enough dinner for both of us."

The word "dinner" echoed in the Boy's head. Even though it was early afternoon and much too early for dinner, the word itself sounded wonderful. The Boy began to climb down, scraping off little pieces of bark as he descended. He got to the last overhanging branch and hung down with his hands, letting go and dropping to the ground.

He brushed himself off and walked over to the park bench. The man motioned toward a blanket spread on the ground. It was covered with the most delicious looking food the Boy had ever seen, laid out in rows. There was every kind of food imaginable – meats, vegetables, desserts, drinks, all looking like pictures in food magazines.

"Come and eat," said the man.

The Boy gaped, for it looked like a wedding feast or something. There was enough food for half the neighborhood. "Where's everybody else?" the Boy asked, looking around.

"Oh, it's just us," answered the man.

"But you don't even know me," said the Boy.

"Oh, yes I do," said the man. "I know everything about you."

"But how?"

"Never mind that for now. Let's eat first."

The Boy had to admit that eating first sounded like just the right thing to do. He sat down on the blanket and the two of them dug in.

Twenty minutes later, the Boy leaned back on his hands and sighed. It had been the best meal of his life. He had never tasted anything more delicious, and as much as he had tried, he hadn't found room for all the great tasting foods that had been laid out before him. Best of all, even though he was very full, he wasn't uncomfortable. If he had to pick a word, he would say that above all, he felt . . . satisfied.

"Thanks," he said.

"You're welcome," answered the man. "You can have this meal anytime you want."

"Won't I get fat?" asked the Boy.

The man laughed out loud and the sound was like music echoing around the tops of the trees. "No, you won't get fat. You can eat as much as you want. Whenever you want. It will always be here. All you have to do is to be hungry."

"I don't understand," said the Boy.

"There's nothing to understand," said the man. "You get hungry, I serve you food. That's why I'm called the Server."

"The Server?" asked the Boy.

"Yep. The Server. It's what I like to do best."

"But how much does it cost?" asked the Boy, suddenly becoming suspicious.

The Server laughed again, but this time his laugh held a tinge of sadness. "It doesn't cost anything. It's completely free. And anyone in the whole world can have it whenever they get hungry. The same food you're eating right now."

"But nothing in this world is free," said the Boy. He'd heard his father say that about a million times.

"You're right," answered the Server. "Nothing in this world is free. But the meal I serve you is."

Well, the Boy didn't quite understand how all of that could be. And he did wonder how many other people had found out about the Server. He had a strong urge to tell as many of them as would listen. This was a great deal.

He left the Server and went home, thinking about how good the food had tasted.

So he kept on eating. For the next year, whenever the Boy felt hunger gnawing away at his insides, the Server would show up. Sometimes it was in the park like that first time, and sometimes it was in the middle of the night as the Boy lay in his bed and couldn't sleep. Even in the depths of winter, when the neighborhood streets turned to ice, the Server would show up with warm, steaming bowls of food. And each time, it would taste like the most delicious meal the Boy had ever eaten. He took joy in each and every bite and actually looked forward to getting hungry.

And, gradually, he began to tell some of his friends about the Server. Some of them laughed at him and said that nothing could be so easy. But some of them listened and found the Server themselves. Occasionally they all shared meals together.

But then spring came and everything changed.

It was one of the first warm days of the year and a south wind blew softly through the neighborhood. Buds appeared on trees and lawnmowers could be heard from down the block. The Boy was walking to school when he noticed that someone had set up a little food stand by the edge of the park. A sign proclaimed:

FOOD FROM THE SERVER. GET IT HERE!

The Boy walked up and scratched his head. A man was behind a table piled high with food. It looked a lot like the food the Server had been giving him, but the man was not the same.

"You're not the Server," said the Boy.

"No, I'm not," said the man. "But I'm here to serve you just like he does. I've tweaked the recipes a little. If you thought that the food tasted good before, you should taste it now. Here, check it out."

The man handed him a small morsel of food on a toothpick. The Boy took it and popped it into his mouth. It tasted delicious – a lot like what the Server gave him, but subtly different. There seemed to be a few different spices in it and some subtle flavors the Boy couldn't identify. It appealed to his sense of adventure.

"Cool," he said. "This is good."

"Yes it is," answered the man smiling. "And it comes right from the Server. But I tweaked it just a little. I've been studying all my life about this. One whole wall of my house is stacked with cookbooks. I can make the food that comes from the Server even more perfect."

"I'll take a plate," said the Boy.

"Great," said the man. "That'll be five dollars."

"Five dollars?" said the Boy. "But the food from the Server is free."

"Yes it is," answered the man smoothly. "But like I said, I've got a whole wall full of cookbooks. Those books weren't free. I really want to share what I've learned. But I gotta make a living."

The Boy thought about walking away. After all, he was right at the edge of the park where he'd first met the Server. But the delicious looking food was right in front of him and he was feeling hungry. Maybe this would be even better. He dug his school lunch money out of his pocket and handed it to the man.

The boy sat down on a park bench and ate. The food was indeed delicious. When he finished he licked his lips and thought about getting another plate, because his hunger wasn't quite satisfied. But he didn't have any more money.

"Come back tomorrow," called the man as the Boy left the park. "I'm cooking up something even better."

By the time the Boy got to school he was hungry again.

The next day was Saturday and the Boy didn't have to go to school. The night before, he had lain awake thinking of the man with all the cookbooks. He wondered what exotic, delicious food he would dream up next. The Server was great, no doubt about that, he reminded himself. But anyone could go to the Server. Anyone in the whole world.

But that guy in the park yesterday was only one man and he had secret recipes.

The Boy couldn't wait to taste more secret recipe food. So the next morning he opened his piggy bank and took out another five dollars.

"Here ya' go," said the Boy, handing the money to the man at the park. The food smells were even more tempting than the day before.

The man took the Boy's money and frowned. "It's $7.50 today," he said.

"Seven fifty? Why?" asked the Boy.

"These recipes take more expensive ingredients. But they're worth it. Here, have a taste."

The man handed the Boy a toothpick. He sampled the food and, indeed, it was delicious. There were several more exotic spices that the Boy hadn't tasted before. He knew he had to have a whole plate of it. But he'd only brought five dollars.

"Tell you what," said the man. "If you do a few chores for me, I'll give you the plate for only five bucks."

"What kind of chores?" asked the Boy.

"Oh, just some small things. Run your bike up to the store and get some groceries. But you gotta get just the right ingredients in just the right order from just the right store. And there are a lot of stores out there."

"Okay," said the Boy. "I can handle that."

Then the man stuck out his hand and said, "Welcome to my little operation, kid. They call me the Chef."

He handed the Boy a fistful of papers, all with lists of ingredients and highly detailed instructions on how to tell that each ingredient was just the right one, had just the right amount of ripeness, was just the right size, etc., etc., etc. And each ingredient had to come from a different store. The Boy read the lists and frowned. How would he ever get this right?

"Don't fret, kid," said the Chef. "Just do the best you can and I'm sure you'll get it eventually. It took me most of a lifetime."

The Boy gritted his teeth and hopped on his bike. He felt butterflies in his stomach as he rode, not wanting to disappoint such an obviously learned man as the Chef. It took him two hours to gather all the ingredients from all the different stores, and even then he wasn't sure he had gotten any of them right.

"Good job, kid," said the Chef as the Boy pulled up at the park, the groceries in his basket. "Now let's cook it all up. And since you did so much work for me, I won't even charge you for the plate this time."

That sounded good to the Boy, for by now he was feeling more hungry then he had ever been in his life. He couldn't wait to dive into the food that would undoubtedly be delicious, a meal like no one else in the world had ever tasted. The Chef set to work with pots and pans and camp stoves. In an hour, the food was ready.

The Boy sat down on the blanket. As he took his first bite, he frowned and nearly spit it out of his mouth. It didn't taste terrible. In fact, it didn't taste like much at all. It was simply bland. What had happened to the exotic flavors from yesterday? He looked up at the Chef in dismay.

"Not so good, huh?" asked the Chef. "I guess you didn't

quite get the right ingredients. But don't worry. I'll go to the store myself. Come back tomorrow and I'll serve you another one of my famous meals. And then you can try again at the store. I like you kid, I really do. I'll make you one of my protégées. Someday you'll learn to be a Chef, just like me."

That night, the Boy went to bed hungry.

And so it went.

For the next several weeks, the Boy would show up with money from his piggy bank every day and buy a meal from the Chef. He would always have to bargain with the man, because each day the food was a little more expensive. And each day the Boy would have to run more and more errands, going to more and more stores. And then they would make a meal together. Each day it would taste a little better, but only a little. Most days the Boy couldn't eat it at all and he went home hungry and disappointed.

One day, the Boy sat on the ground by the Chef with tears in his eyes. He'd failed again. He'd been trying so hard, but he just wasn't making any progress. The Chef knew so much about food and he knew so little. He hung his head and mumbled, "I used to get really good food for free."

The Chef put his hand on the Boy's shoulder. "I know," he said. "Free food is nice, but it's a cruel world. You have to work hard if you want a really good meal. Keep at it. You'll find what you're looking for."

The Boy pulled away and wiped his eyes. What had the Chef said? "You'll find what you're looking for?"

The Boy suddenly remembered that day up in the tree.

He had been looking for something then. And he had found it.

"I gotta go," muttered the Boy.

Within seconds, the Boy was running across the park as fast as his feet could carry him. He found his favorite maple tree and shinnied up the trunk. He grabbed the first overhanging branch and scrambled up the rest of the way, finally resting on his personal perch near the top.

Behind him at the edge of the park, the Chef turned away and shook his head. "Well, I tried," he said to no one in particular. "I guess some people are just never meant to get it."

The Boy looked up into a blue sky flecked with clouds. He felt his heart quicken.

"I'm hungry," he whispered.

"Down here," came the answer.

And sure enough, when the Boy looked down through the branches, the Server was there. A huge feast was spread out on a blanket. The Server was smiling up at him with a face like the sun.

The Boy scrambled back down the tree as fast as he could, nearly falling a few times. But he made it safely down and slowly approached the Server.

"Take. Eat," the Server said.

The Boy sat down and cautiously took his first bite. The food was as good as it had been the first time, maybe even better because he had been eating bland food for so long.

The Boy paused before he put the second bite into is mouth. "So I don't have to run errands to pay for this?" he asked. "I don't have to try and figure out all the ingredients?"

"Never," answered the Server. "You can try to figure out the ingredients if you want. That's not a bad thing and some people love doing that. But the food will always be here when you're hungry. And it will always be free."

That sounded like the best thing the Boy had ever heard. He ate until he was content. And satisfied. At last he sat back and said, "I wonder what it would be like if the whole world could sit down with us here and eat together."

The Server smiled and said, "You have no idea…"

PARABLE 4:
THE ISLAND

There were just eight of us on the sailboat along with the captain. We were having a wonderful voyage. None of us had met before the trip, but we seemed to be getting along just fine. By day, the ocean was a brilliant turquoise; by night, the sky was lit by the Milky Way. We had been blessed with clear weather and a gentle breeze for the entire week thus far. The feeling of being happily lost on the endless ocean was delicious, even though we assumed the captain had been plotting our course all along.

All of us had answered an ad in a travel magazine for singles, so none of us was shy. Every night we'd sit on the deck under the vast canopy of stars. Moments like that, with the splendor of the universe arrayed all around as a backdrop, were conducive to talking about deep, heady things. I didn't usually say much, but I liked to listen and encourage the others. That was just my way.

There was The Crystal Woman. She had quite a collection of rare stones, and even kept one in her shirt pocket, close to her heart. She said that it would protect her from bad karma and help her to live a healthier, longer life. She gave a crystal to me on the first night, holding it out to me as if it were part of the Crown Jewels. I took it and smiled, examining it and nodding, even though I didn't believe in crystals. The last thing I wanted to do was to rub a new friend the wrong way.

There was The Meditator. He would put himself into a trance every evening on one of the deck chairs, repeating a phrase over and over. When he had finished, he would join the rest of us. I once asked him if meditation made him feel better. He nodded his head and offered to teach me, but I said, "Maybe some other time." I didn't want to hurt his feelings by saying that the whole idea of going into a trance made me a little nervous.

The Tarot Card Woman was an older lady who read fortunes at night by the light of the ship's lantern. We all laughed at some of the things she told us about ourselves, though, strangely, some of her guesses were pretty close to the mark. On our third night at sea, it was my turn to have my fortune read. Although it was full of generalities and half-truths, I pretended to be amazed. I didn't want to spoil the fun. And besides, she seemed to think it was more than a game, so who was I to question her beliefs?

I was very popular on that voyage. Everyone seemed to really like me because I knew how to fit right in. I had my own beliefs, of course, but in my mind it would have sounded like preaching to tell the others what I believed. No one likes to be preached at. Besides, I was sure the others had been exposed to my belief system a thousand times before, and they wouldn't be interested, since theirs were so different. The important thing was to tolerate alternative views.

On the fourth night we all stayed up until 5 AM. By then we had gotten really comfortable with each other. We did a lot of talking that night, and even some off-key singing. As things finally broke up and we stood to make our bleary-eyed way to our bunks, I glanced off to the east. The sky was already lightening and I saw a dark sliver on the edge of the horizon. It looked like an island.

****

It's hard to know exactly what happened next. I went to bed of course, just like everyone else, and fell instantly to sleep. But how we all ended up in the water, floundering around like drowning puppies, I'll never know. All I remember is waking to the sounds of shouting, of running feet on the deck above, of someone banging on my cabin door. And I can't forget those terrifying words, "We're sinking!"

I jumped out of bed and ran up to the deck in panic. The boat tilted at a nauseating angle, and as I stood there gaping it felt like I was in a fun-house, the kind where the floors heave up and down. Soon the angle got too steep for me to stand, and although I tried to hang onto the mast, my hand slipped and I fell into the water.

None of us had had time to prepare for something like this. One moment we were sleeping and the next we were in the water. I watched the top of the mast slide beneath the waves and then we were alone in the eerie quiet of the open ocean. I grabbed at a wooden chest that was floating by. I climbed on top of it, hanging on for dear life. I looked around. Others had grabbed onto bits of Styrofoam coolers, pieces of wood planking . . . anything that would float. I counted heads. There were only eight of us; all passengers. The captain was gone.

We paddled toward each other and grabbed hands so we could stay together. We bombarded each other with questions. Did anyone know what had happened? Why did the ship sink? Did the captain go down with the ship? But none of us knew a thing.

"What should we do?" someone asked.

"Maybe we should stay together," said someone else. "The captain might have sent out a distress signal before we went down."

"I don't think so," said another. "Had he been able to do that, he would have made it off the boat like the rest of us. We need to figure out which way to go. There must be an island around here someplace."

"But which way?" asked someone else.

We were having trouble staying together because the waves kept trying to separate us. I sputtered and tasted harsh salt-water. Others coughed.

"Hold onto my arm," said The Crystal Woman to the person next to her. With her other hand she produced a stone from her shirt pocket. The rising sun caught its surface and turned it into a shining rainbow, making it seem like a magical omen of great power. She squeezed the stone in her palm and closed her eyes. "I can feel the vibrations," she said. "The crystal is telling us there is an island to the north."

I gritted my teeth as I hung onto the wooden chest. North? I was sure I had seen an island to the east, just as we were all going to bed. At least I was pretty sure. But I didn't speak up. The woman was so sure of her belief in crystals; besides, I might be mistaken.

"Not north," said The Tarot Card Woman. "We need to go west." She seemed to have gone into some sort of psychic trance. She took a deep, spooky breath and pointed to the west with her long finger.

I looked to the west and saw only waves. I looked toward the east, where the sun was just rising out of the ocean. I couldn't see any sign of land. Maybe I was too low in the water. Or maybe there wasn't any land to see that way at all.

"South," said The Meditator. "The universe is directing us to the south. I can see a flaming arrow in the water." We all looked that way. I saw only more waves.

My mind was a jumble. Should I tell the others what I had seen? All three who had spoken were convinced they were right. If I gave my opinion, then I would be saying they were wrong. Who was I to judge their beliefs? So I kept quiet.

"Well, it's clear to me what we should do," said a fourth person, a Lawyer. "Each of us should follow the person we think has the right answer."

We all nodded our heads. This seemed very reasonable. We all had a free choice, after all. Choice was the important thing. We would each decide for ourselves.

We let go of each other's hands and began to drift apart. The Lawyer followed The Crystal Woman. Two others followed The Meditator. Another followed The Tarot Card Woman. That left me. The others looked back as they bobbed in the waves.

"What about you?" shouted The Lawyer.

"I'll go toward the sun," I yelled back. I couldn't stop thinking about that smudge I had seen on the horizon. "To the east." The others smiled and wished me luck. We all were so enlightened, allowing each other to make up our own mind.

Everyone drifted out of sight and I was all alone. I turned toward the east and began paddling. At first, all I saw ahead of me was endless ocean. I felt incredibly small. I began to get thirsty. Very thirsty.

After an hour of paddling, a wave lifted me high and I thought I saw a gray smudge on the horizon. After ten more minutes of paddling another wave lifted me. The smudge had grown larger and I knew it was an island. I cheered and paddled harder.

But then I thought of the others. I spun around, trying to see if any of them was still in view. But I saw no one. I shouted at the top of my lungs, but all I heard in response was the sound of the rolling waves. I shook my head and went back to my paddling. They had made their choice and I had made mine.

Near sundown, I finally reached the shore of a beautiful

island. The breeze had died down and gentle waves eased me onto a sandy shore. There was a man there, standing in front of a blazing fire. He wore a simple, white robe and sandals.

As I climbed unsteadily to my feet, the man smiled and held out his arms. "Welcome," he said. "You must be hungry."

I gratefully wolfed down the piece of fish he offered me, along with some bread that he had broken off from what tasted like a fresh loaf. I took the flask of cool, clear water he handed me, sure that such a small amount could never quench my enormous thirst. But as I kept drinking and drinking and drinking, the flask remained full, as if it were connected to an artesian well.

My thirst quenched, I sat down on the sand, feeling refreshed and clean. I noticed that my clothes were suddenly, inexplicably dry, and the warmth from the fire felt heavenly. I started to ask the man where we were, what island this was, but he walked away from me. He stopped at the water's edge and stood looking out to sea. The sun splashed below the western horizon. Soon it was dark and stars filled the sky.

"What are you looking for?" I called.

"The others," he answered.

"Others?"

"Yes, there were seven more with you in the water."

My breath caught in my throat. How could he have known that? The man came over and looked into my eyes. His own eyes danced in the firelight.

"Well," I stammered. "They went different ways – each

of them. It was each person's choice."

"Yes, it was," he said. "So why did you come this way?"

"I saw land to the east, a few hours before the ship went down."

"So you knew the right way to go," he said. He didn't sound angry or accusing. So why did I feel so uneasy?

"Well . . . I guess so," I managed to say. "But I didn't want to judge them. They were all so sure they were right."

"But you knew the Way," he said again.

I looked out at the inky blackness of the ocean. I thought of what it would feel like to be out there still, bobbing in the dark. I considered going back out, swimming all night, somehow, trying to find the others so I could bring them to this shore.

"It's too late," the man said, as if reading my thoughts.

"What?"

"It's too late to save them. They're gone."

I knew in my heart that he was right. I watched the gentle waves lap the sand, as tears welled up in my eyes.

The man put his hand on my shoulder. I looked up and his smile was warm. "I'm so glad you're here," he said. "You need to rest now. You've had a very long day."

He led me to a place on the beach that had obviously been prepared in advance. A robe, like the man's, was folded at the head of my resting place, in the shape of a pillow. A flask of my own sat beside it. I lay down on my back and looked up at the glittering stars. It was a long, long time before I was able to sleep.

PARABLE 5:
THE RUNNER

The Runner first raised himself to his feet when he was very small. "Hey! Look what I can do!" he said. He looked down at his feet, clad in baby-sized tennis shoes. He'd seen his feet before when he was lying on his back and kicking his legs in the air. He could even put his toes in his mouth. But this was something different. His feet seemed to be far below him as he planted them firmly on the road. Well, not firmly, because he was wobbling, but firmly enough. And he had let go of the crib he had been holding onto. But the best was yet to come.

He gingerly lifted one small foot and moved it a forward a couple inches. Then he moved the other. And then the first one again. He was walking! Before long the crib was far behind him. He looked ahead and saw something in the road. It looked like a table.

"Hey! What's that?" he shouted. "I wanna see that!"

He moved his little feet faster. Now, instead of simply placing one foot in front of the other, he jumped on the balls of his feet.

"Whoa!" he shouted. "I'm running! And I never want to stop!"

He looked down as he ran, marveling at the way his legs moved, at the way his feet pounded the pavement. *I have the best legs in the world*, he thought.

He quickly arrived at the table he'd been racing toward. On it was a children's book. "Cool," he said, grabbing it as he ran on by.

He read the book as he raced along, looking at every picture on every page, occasionally glancing up to make sure he wouldn't run into anything. When he was finished, he tossed the book aside and looked ahead. He could see more tables along the road, one right after another, each with a book. He grabbed them all and looked at each one in turn.

"I love this," he said in a voice that had suddenly become stronger. He looked down at his marvelous, pumping legs, and noticed that his shoes were no longer baby shoes, but had grown into little boy tennies with pictures of baseballs on each toe.

"Cool," he said as he kept on running.

Suddenly there was someone running beside him. He was the same height, but he had a grown man's face.

"Hi!" the man said.

"Who are you?" asked The Runner.

"I'm The Supervisor of the Race," answered the man.

"What's that?"

"I'm here to see if anybody has trouble running. If they do, I can help them."

"Cool," said The Runner. "But I don't need any help. Check out these legs." He kicked into higher gear and zoomed ahead, leaving The Supervisor far behind, smiling.

Further down the road, after he had read at least a thousand books, his feet had grown much larger. He was wearing a pair of spotless, white gym shoes and a baggy pair of dark blue shorts that showed off his muscular legs.

Suddenly he was surrounded by a group of other runners on the road, racing along and matching him stride for stride. They were all his age and they were laughing.

"What an idiot!" they shouted at him. "You think you're fast, don't you? Well you're not. You're slower than all of us."

"No I'm not," answered The Runner. And he kicked it into another gear and left some of them in the dust. But not all of them. Some of them actually raced ahead and he couldn't catch them.

For the first time in his life, The Runner felt his heart sink. The joy of running diminished for just a moment and he struggled to catch his breath. But it only took a moment to shake it off.

If anyone else had passed him at that moment, they would have seen a slight redness in the calf muscles of his legs. And they would have noticed that he wasn't traveling as quickly as he had been moments before. And they would have seen that he was now carrying a small backpack.

But The Runner didn't notice any of that. As he looked down at his legs, he couldn't see his calf muscles. And he didn't feel the backpack, for it was very small.

"I love this," he said. "I love running."

Suddenly, The Supervisor was there again by his side. Nothing about him had changed. "Need any help?" he shouted.

"No," answered The Runner. "I'm fine." And he was. So The Supervisor slowed down and faded back into the distance.

When he found a girlfriend, The Runner was really happy. Now he was no longer running alone. Oh, he'd never been completely alone of course. He had a family – a mother and father, two brothers and a sister, and friends who cheered him on. But a girlfriend was a different thing altogether. He could share everything with her. As they ran along together they talked and talked, holding hands and reading books out loud. But when they came to a fork in the road, they went in different directions and he was alone again.

Later, if anyone had passed him by, they would have seen a grimace on his face, and a new swelling on his right knee, along with lumps on his calf muscles. They would have noticed trickles of blood from a skinned elbow that had never healed. He'd gotten it when he'd fallen, just after his girlfriend left. And his backpack was larger. But The Runner didn't notice any of that. He had put the fall completely out of his mind. That was his way. For how could you get anywhere if you kept stopping to feel sorry for yourself?

The Supervisor was beside him again. "Doin' okay?" he asked.

The Runner clenched his teeth. "Of course I'm okay. Why do you keep coming around here checking on me? Can't you see I'm trying to get somewhere? Why don't you just leave me alone?"

The Supervisor frowned. "But your knee," he said. "I can get you a brace for that."

The Runner gaped. "My knee? What's wrong with my knee? You must be blind. Can't you see I'm running better than ever?"

And he raced on alone.

The Runner went to college, happily devouring every book he found by the side of the road. The only thing that slowed him up was a piece of terrible news he received one day.

His mother had come up from behind him. "I have to tell you something," she said. "There's been a terrible accident. Your brother fell off the road."

The Runner slowed down for the first time in his life and stared. "Fell off the road? But that's impossible!"

But it wasn't impossible. And now his older brother was gone forever

The Runner tried to think of something to say, some way to comfort his mother and maybe himself. But he didn't know how. So he simply ran on ahead, shaking his head. "Nobody's supposed to fall off the road," he muttered. "Not until they're old. Then they're at the end anyways."

Later, if anyone had passed him by, they would have seen that his left ankle was now at a funny angle and had begun to swell up. They would have seen that both his knees were skinned from the fall he took just after his mother had given him the news. They would have noticed him wheezing occasionally. And his backpack had grown to the size of a small suitcase. But The Runner didn't notice any of that.

"Are you okay?" came a voice from his side. It was The Supervisor again.

"Go away!" shouted The Runner, slowing down just for a moment. "Why do you keep on showing up? I don't want you here. What good are you anyway? Aren't you supposed to be supervising or something? Why weren't you supervising my brother?"

There was silence along the road as both of them stopped and looked at each other. The Supervisor's normally kind face fell and he looked down at the ground. "I'm sorry about your brother," he said.

"A lot of good that does," answered The Runner. "You know, come to think of it, I bet you aren't The Supervisor at all. I don't think there even is a supervisor. We're all alone out here, running along the road."

"That's not true," answered The Supervisor.

"Yes it is," answered The Runner, and he took off down the road again, sure that he didn't need a supervisor, even if there really was one.

And then he found company on his run. He fell in love and got married. The two of them ran along the road together and it seemed as if the days were all sunny and the nights were all filled with stars. This was so much better than running alone.

Then came the children, three beautiful runners. He and his wife taught the little ones their first steps, eventually showing them how to run on their own. Sometimes they ran ahead, sometimes behind. But always the family was together.

"This must be the best time ever," said The Runner. And it was.

But one day The Runner's mother caught up with them on the road. She was gasping. "Wait up for a second," she said.

"Come on, Mom," said The Runner. "Keep up! You gotta see what the kids are up to now!"

But his mother couldn't keep up. She was staggering and The Runner slowed down to see what was going on. He almost had to stop.

"Mom?" asked the runner. "Are you okay?"

But his mother fell to her knees, head drooping. The Runner felt his insides go weak. He reached down his hand. "Let me help you," he said.

His mother looked up with a wistful smile. "You can't help me," she said. "I have to leave the road."

"But you can't do that!" gasped The Runner.

"It's been a wonderful race," she said. "And I've been truly blessed all these years. But now it's time to go home."

"Home?" he sputtered. "What home? There is no home! There's only the road. And you have to keep running."

His mother simply shook her head. He tried to take her up in his arms. If she couldn't run on her own, he would carry her. But to his dismay, he found that he could only lift her slightly off the pavement. As he kept on trying to lift, her eyes closed and her breathing became shallow. Finally, she stopped breathing all together and rolled out of his arms and off the side of the road.

"No!" he screamed. But it was too late. His mother was gone.

He did the only thing he could think of. He rounded up his wife and children and they all took off running again.

Later, if you had seen him going along, playing with his children and holding hands with his wife, you would have noticed that both his knees were swollen to almost double their size. His ankles were black and blue. His calf muscles looked like knotted ropes. There were bruises all over his body from the falls that were coming more and more frequently. And the backpack had grown huge, stooping him over like an old man.

But The Runner didn't see any of that. In his mind, he was moving like always. When he looked down, he saw a strong, muscular pair of legs. He saw feet that were wearing the latest hi-tech pair of running shoes. And his will was strong enough that he convinced his family to see the same thing.

And all of that worked just fine.

Until one day, when it all fell apart.

He was admiring the view of the forest and the mountains. His wife and children were running on ahead in the road, calling back to him. "Come on, Dad!" they shouted. He smiled and laughed and picked up his pace. But suddenly, his feet wouldn't work. He looked down and saw them tangled up like pipe cleaners. He fell to the ground, bruising his forehead on the pavement. He shook his head to clear it and tried to laugh it off. He got to his feet and stood there wobbling.

Looking down at his legs in horror, he realized he didn't know what to do next. He tried to take a step but his legs tangled again and he fell once more to the pavement. He sat there in the road, gasping.

His wife and family were there in a moment. "What's wrong?" they asked.

"Nothing," he said, keeping a brave face in front of his children. "Just a charley horse, I think. Go on ahead. I'll catch up."

But he couldn't catch up. He could only sit there in the road.

He tried everything. He massaged his legs to try and get them to work. He talked to himself. "Come on, this is ridiculous," he said. "You never needed help before."

And strangely enough, when he looked down at his legs he couldn't see anything wrong. They were perfect, same as always. But whenever he tried to stand, they got tangled up and he fell back down.

He tried crawling, but that was much too slow.

And then the nighttime came.

For his whole life, he had always set his sights on something in the distance – a book, a job, a family. But now, as the sun set and the road ahead darkened, he couldn't see anything at all. He heard night birds squawking in the trees. And he began to shiver.

He stayed there for a long time, teeth chattering. It was only his bull-headedness that kept him from calling for help. He had relied on his own legs forever it seemed, so why should he change?

But his legs had finally given out, and he knew it.

"Hey!" he shouted to the dark night. "Is anyone there? I think I need help."

The Supervisor was there in an instant, bending down next to him. "Did you say you needed help?" he asked.

The Runner could just make out The Supervisor's face, because the sky in the east had begun to lighten. "Where did you come from?" he asked.

"I've been here all along."

The Supervisor stood up straight and stretched. "You've been having a hard time," he said.

The Runner wanted to deny it, like he had been denying things for so long. But this time he couldn't so he simply nodded his head.

"I have to show you something," said The Supervisor. "And it's not going to be pretty."

By now the sun had come up. The day was cloudy, but the ambient light made everything clear. "Can you get to your feet?" asked the Supervisor.

"I don't think so," answered The Runner.

"Then let me help you."

The Supervisor reached down his hand, but The Runner hesitated to take it. Finally, he reached out and let The Supervisor help him to his feet. He stood there wobbling.

"Okay," said The Supervisor. "This is not going to be easy for you. It might be one of the hardest things you'll ever do."

"What?" asked The Runner, feeling a lump form in his

throat.

"There's something you need to see."

The Supervisor produced a large mirror from behind his back. He held it up to The Runner. "Look," he said.

The Runner looked.

What he saw in the mirror made him gasp in sheer terror. For he could see his entire reflection and it wasn't anything like what he had expected to see. Instead of a strong, vital, perfect Runner's body, with muscular legs thick enough to carry him to the end of the road, his legs were spindly and crooked, with knees swollen like rotten apples. His ankles were black and blue, and bent at impossible angles. His elbows were bruised and battered from a multitude of falls. The skin on his face was raw, red, and windblown from the winter wind. But worst of all were his eyes. Instead of the confident eyes he'd always assumed he possessed, he had the eyes of a scared rabbit. And they were filling up with tears.

Suddenly, The Runner felt a huge weight on his back. Still looking into the mirror, he turned sideways and saw an impossibly large backpack, the kind hikers wear when they're doing a trek that will last for many months. And the weight was dragging him back down.

"Help me," he whispered.

The Supervisor started to lift the weight off his back. "Wait!" said The Runner. "I'm not sure what's in there. Maybe it's something I need."

The Supervisor let go. "When you're ready to give it to me, let me know," he said. "I'd like to carry it for you. But I won't take it if you don't want me to."

"What's in there?" asked The Runner.

"I can help you unpack it so you can find out. But eventually, you'll still have to let me carry some of it. Maybe all of it."

"I don't understand," said The Runner. "Where are we going?"

"To The Finish Line," answered The Supervisor. "It's where you've been heading all this time."

"But what's there?"

"It's the most beautiful place. Your mother is there. And so is your brother."

"Can we go there now?" pleaded The Runner.

"In your own time," answered The Supervisor. "You still have a long run ahead of you."

The Runner looked down at his legs. He saw the same thing he'd seen in the mirror – the swollen knees, the spindly calves, the ruined ankles. "But I can't run any more," he said.

"Yes, you can," answered The Supervisor. And he reached out and touched one of the knees. The swelling immediately went down. The Runner could feel warm blood flowing through the joint. "Can you heal all of me?" he asked.

"Eventually," said The Supervisor. "But you'll have to help me do it."

"How?" asked The Runner.

"I'll teach you," answered The Supervisor. "But first you have to let me carry that backpack, at least for awhile."

The Runner gritted his teeth. It took all of his willpower to let go of the pack, but he finally took the straps off. The

Supervisor took the pack and grunted, putting it on his own back.

"When can we open it?" asked The Runner.

"Maybe at the next bend in the road," answered The Supervisor. "But we'll have to stop for awhile to do that. Is that okay?"

"I think so," answered The Runner, though he had never liked to stop at any time in his whole life.

The Runner got to his feet, feeling somewhat lighter, but still very shaky. He now remembered what he had to do to make his legs move forward. He might not be able to run yet, but at least he could walk.

Then the two of them set out down the road, one of them limping and wheezing, and the other carrying a huge and heavy pack. Eventually, they got to the next bend in the road. And for the first time in his life, The Runner sat down for a rest. . . .

PARABLE 6:
THE RIVER

L ong ago he had floated down the River with his wife and ended up here. But it was so long ago, he didn't remember much about where he had come from. All that was important was that the River had dropped them here to start a new life together. That had been good enough. More than good enough. It had been perfect.

The place the River had dropped them was beautiful. As a young married couple they had explored every inch of the land, the acres and acres of forest, the sweeping meadows, the hills, the valleys. He built a small cabin on top of the highest hill and planted the first crops in the meadow while his wife worked to turn the little cabin into a home. Within that first year, they were able to settle in as if the land had been made just for them. The first year's crop was abundant. There was sweet water just below the surface for their wells. There were freshwater ponds filled with trout and bass. There was more than enough firewood to last a lifetime. So they prospered.

The end of that first year found them sitting on their front porch at sunset, gazing off to the west.

"Does it get any better than this?" he asked his wife, holding her hand.

She simply shook her head and smiled, and he thought he saw a tear forming at the corner of her eye.

He gazed out over the land, turning scarlet now with the setting sun – the trees, the fields, the valleys, and far, far in the distance, the black line of the River. For some reason, when his eyes fell upon that faint black line, he felt queasy in the pit of his stomach. Yes, the River had brought them here only a year ago. But his cabin and his fields were in the very middle of his lands, and in all of his wanderings, he had avoided venturing too close to the water. For even from a distance, he could see that the River moved very fast. And if it had brought them here in the first place, it could take them away again. And he never wanted that to happen.

****

One day his wife gave birth to a son. As he felt the baby's tiny, tiny hand wrap around his little finger, he felt prouder than he ever had felt in his life. For he knew that his son would grow up on this land, the three of them to-gether making a family. And someday his son would find a wife and raise a family of his own, right here on the same land.

So where would his son's wife come from? There were only the three of them on the land. He supposed she would have to come from the family of one of the Visitors, the people who floated down from upriver and landed here occasionally. They'd made friends with quite a few of them since they had settled here, but Visitors never stayed long. All of them seemed to have an urge to climb back in the River and move on.

But he would never do that because the world he had made was perfect. Besides, he was becoming afraid of the water.

And then their daughter was born and things got even better. They had the ideal family – a father and a mother and a son and a daughter. Along with their son taking over for his father on the land, someday the daughter would also marry, and she too would raise her family on this land. And then there would be grandchildren.

****

The years went by much faster than he would have preferred. But they were good years. That's not to say there weren't some difficulties. Sometimes the rains didn't come and sometimes they came too much. Sometimes the winters were harsh. Sometimes insects tried to destroy their crops. But they were diligent, the four of them, and they celebrated each season in its turn.

It was when his son turned seven that he noticed something disquieting. He was sitting on the porch at sunset as usual, holding his son in his lap. He gazed out at his land like a king surveying his domain. But on this day, the thin dark line of the River looked a little thicker than it had before. Was the River moving closer? He tried not to think about that. But it was like telling himself not to think about a purple fish. He couldn't help it. From then on he kept a watchful eye on that thin, black line, the one that was definitely getting thicker with each passing day. And one day he decided to go down there and see for himself.

It wasn't easy to travel down and down through the woods to the River. As he got closer and could smell the rich green odor of the water ahead, every fiber of his body wanted him to turn back. But he kept going because this was his land, his perfect place, and he needed to know what was happening.

He came around a bend in the trail and gasped. One entire acre of trees had been flooded out by the rushing River. Oaks, maples, cottonwoods, all of them had deep, dark water swirling halfway up their trunks. In the distance, he could see whole trees floating downstream from other sections of his land.

In his fright, he simply turned away and ran up the hill. He vowed to forget what he had just seen. But he knew that whatever happened next, his perfect world would never be the same again.

****

On his son's tenth birthday, they were all sitting around

the kitchen table having a party. The boy took a huge bite of birthday cake and smiled, frosting oozing out from between his teeth. "When can we go in the River?" he asked.

His father's jaw dropped. His son's question had come out of the blue. "Why would you ever want to do that?"

"To see what's downstream," answered the boy. "That's where the Visitors always go. None of them know what's down there, but they jump in anyways."

The father put down his fork. "That's because they don't have their own land. So they think they can do better someplace else. But we have everything we need right here."

"But didn't you and Mom float here from upstream?"

"Don't ever ask that again," answered the father firmly. His son pouted and the father felt bad to see the hurt on his boy's face. But he knew that sometimes you just had to lay down the law, and there were some things you didn't talk about.

****

The son was fifteen and the daughter was twelve. The father was feeling more and more uneasy as the days went on, one after the other. Sometimes his son would disappear on long walks around the land. The father didn't know for sure, but he thought that the boy was wandering down to the River, even though he'd been absolutely forbidden to do so. The father knew he should follow his son to see for sure, but his fear of the water had now become a living, dark thing inside his head. The River had continued to ex-

67

pand and it had engulfed another whole section of forest. All of the lower potato fields were now under water. And there was nothing anyone could do about it.

Visitors continued to come. The father tried to discourage them as much as he could. In the early days he had been a gracious host. Not anymore. Because every time any Visitors left, his son, his daughter, and even his wife grew melancholy. All three of them would get a distant look in their eyes and gaze longingly down at the River, which could now be seen clearly from the front porch of the house.

One night in bed, his wife said to him, "Maybe we can't stay here forever. Maybe we should go and see what's downstream. We did it once before."

He hadn't even been able to answer.

His daughter, being twelve and already much more forthright than he would have cared for, said one night over dinner, "All my friends among the Visitors have gone down the River. Can I go, too?"

He'd sent her to bed without supper.

Even his son, who always wanted to please his father, sometimes used a roundabout way to broach the subject. He'd say something like, "I wonder if the water in the River is very cold."

All the father could answer was, "You don't even know how to swim."

****

His son was eighteen and his daughter was fifteen. Things

had deteriorated much further. It was a genuine crisis. The River was only fifty yards below the house, lapping at the bottom of the hill. The cornfields were gone. The forests were gone. The silos were flooded halfway up and some of them had tipped over and fallen into the rushing water. Behind them to the east, the River had engulfed everything as well, so they were trapped on a small, raised island.

The father gaped down from the front porch at the rushing River below. They were still high and dry in the house, and they had stored enough food in the attic to last them a long time, but the water was still rising. His family stood around him. It was a beautiful, warm, sunny day. But instead of green fields below, there was only water, water, and more water.

His wife gently took his hand and said the unthinkable. "I think it's time to go."

He gasped. "No it's not. We're still okay."

"Not for long," she said, her lips tight. "We have to jump in the River and float downstream before it comes up here and gets us."

He recoiled in horror. "Float? Nobody's gonna float in water like that. Do you see how fast it's moving? We'll all drown."

His wife sighed. They had been having this argument over and over for a whole year. "The Visitors didn't drown," she said. "Sometimes I watched them float away and they were smiling."

"That's because they didn't have their own place to settle," he said. "We do."

"Not for long," she answered.

"The River will recede," he said. "It'll go away and leave us alone so we can stay here forever. Just like we always planned."

"I don't think so," his wife said.

"But I want to stay here!" he shouted. "I can't leave!" Tears streamed down his cheeks.

His kids were shocked to see their father cry so openly. Nobody spoke.

Finally, his wife broke the silence. "We're leaving," she said simply, "all of us. We have to go downstream. If you won't come, then the kids and I will go by ourselves."

He stopped crying as abruptly as he had started. He sputtered, "But . . . you can't take the kids."

"There's no other choice," she said.

"But I'm their father," he answered.

"And I'm their mother. And I know they can't stay here. We want you to come with us. We want that with every fiber in our bodies. But if you refuse, we're going without you. Now."

He couldn't think of an answer. He simply clenched his fists and turned away. His wife grabbed the hands of the kids and walked them down the steps of the porch. He couldn't bear to look.

He knew he should try to follow. He should chase them down and pull them back up to the house. But he found he couldn't move. Because maybe his wife was right. And he still was much too afraid of the water.

Before his wife and kids reached the River, he turned and went into the house. Alone.

****

One week later the water had risen enough to lap at the steps of the front porch. He was sitting alone at the kitchen table in the tomblike silence, trying to eat a sandwich. Abandoned, bitter and lonely, he knew the water would be inside the house soon. And then it would kill him.

There was a knock at his door.

It startled him so much that he dropped the remains of his sandwich. He stared as the knock came again. Who could it be? The only place anyone could have come from was the River.

He got to his feet and made his way slowly to the door. A man was standing on his porch in some sort of wet suit. He had long, dark hair, soaking wet and clinging to his head. His feet were bare.

"May I come in?" the stranger asked.

The man was so stunned that he could only open the door and wave the stranger in.

The stranger entered and closed the door behind him. He held out his hand. "I'm the Lifeguard," the man said.

"Lifeguard?"

"Yes, and I've come to get you out of here."

"But I don't want to leave."

The Lifeguard looked up at the ceiling. "It's time for you to make a leap of faith. The River is coming for you whether you want it to or not."

The man looked toward the door. "How did you get here?" he asked.

"I swam up from downstream," answered the Lifeguard.

The man shook his head. That was impossible. No one ever came from downstream. The River only flowed one way. "Nobody can do that," he said.

"I can," the Lifeguard answered. And his eyes were so warm, so sincere, that it was hard not to believe him.

"Have you seen my family?" the man asked, for he was feeling a tiny twinge of hope. Maybe they hadn't drowned after all.

The Lifeguard didn't answer. Instead, he asked some questions of his own. "Do you remember floating down the River, long ago when you came here? Do you remember the excitement you felt when you first jumped in?"

A few, long dormant feelings entered the man's mind, but he pushed them back down. He shook his head and looked at the floor.

"I remember," the Lifeguard continued. "You were a good swimmer, and fearless. You couldn't wait to see what was around the next bend. Then you found this place and forgot about all of that. But the River kept moving."

The man looked up. "But I don't want it to keep moving. Why can't it just stop? Why can't it go away and leave me be? Why can't it just turn into an ocean or something, and hold still?"

The Lifeguard paused. "There is an ocean," he said. "With a shoreline more beautiful than anything you could ever imagine. But you have to float down the River to get there."

"Is my family there?"

"That's something you have to find out for yourself. But I came here to help."

At that moment, the front door crashed inward and a wall of dark water rushed in. The man was swept backwards, his body hitting the far wall, his head going under. His arms pin wheeled as he tried to push himself above the water. The water receded for a moment and swept him out through the front door and into the River, now up to the level of the house. His head surfaced and he flailed away, sputtering and trying to stay above water.

Suddenly he felt a strong hand grabbing him under his armpit. "Hold on to me," said the Lifeguard, and he was lifted up so his head stayed above the surface. He looked back and saw his house, already far behind them, collapsing into the River. Tears came to his eyes and mixed with the splashing waves. "All those years gone," he muttered.

The Lifeguard put his free hand on the man's shoulder as they floated. "There are more good years ahead," he said softly.

"How can you know something like that?" asked the man. He was beginning to relax a little, for by now, he knew that he wasn't going to drown. The Lifeguard's hand was strong. And even when the Lifeguard eased his grip, the man's own body was buoyant enough to keep him afloat.

"I made this River," answered the Lifeguard. "I know what's behind and what's ahead. I know the entire River, all the way down to the ocean."

"Did my family make it?" asked the man, now craning his head to try and look around the next bend.

The Lifeguard looked full into his eyes. "Your wife and your son and your daughter all know how to swim," he said. "And now you do too."

The Lifeguard let go. There was a moment of real panic

as the man began to flail. But he didn't go under. He found that by kicking his legs in a certain way, he could stay up on his own. He even began to experiment with moving his arms to make himself travel to different sections of the River. The Lifeguard, watching nearby, floated along and smiled. "See? You can do it," he said.

"Are you going to stay here with me?" the man asked.

"I'll be here if you need me," answered the Lifeguard. "But for now I have to go upstream."

The Lifeguard turned, and with powerful strokes, began to swim upstream. The man drifted in the opposite direction, faster and faster, until he could no longer see the Lifeguard. He continued kicking his legs and moving his arms. After awhile, he actually started enjoying himself. And if he had put words to it, he would have said that he felt young again. Because he knew now that he could float in the current for as long as he needed to

He thought that maybe there were some good things downstream after all. Of course there were. His family was down there someplace.

So he did the only thing he could do. He kicked his legs and traveled around the next bend.

PARABLE 7:
THE SINGER

It was an act of worship. She stood up on the hill and sang her heart out. She felt the emotion swell inside her chest, the notes flowing smoothly and reverently. The melody wrapped itself around the words perfectly, like they always did with such a familiar song. But still, the way she sang it was uniquely her own.

Amazing grace, how sweet the sound
That saved a wretch like me. . . .

Like always, the words spoke to her. "That saved a wretch like me." If anyone had ever been a wretch, it was her. She had made one bad life choice after another until she had brought herself down as low as anyone can go. She had dwelt for several years among the lost, the rejected, and the hopelessly broken. But God had lifted her up and washed her clean. Had it been up to people, it would have taken a lifetime of scrubbing to bring her out, no matter how well-meaning the social workers, how wise the counselors, how compassionate the church people. But God had done it in the blinking of an eye.

She paused between verses and took a long, cleansing breath. This was her favorite spot in the world. She stood in front of twin pine trees and heard the breeze blow through the forested hilltop behind her. Below her was the town, laid out like miniature houses and shops in the model train exhibit at the museum she would visit when she was a little girl. She had longed to one day have a neat little house like that. And now she did, for her house was down there, a block away from the bottom of the hill, smoke curling from the chimney and amber light glowing from the windows in the evening dusk.

T'was Grace that taught my heart to fear.
And Grace, my fears relieved.

It truly did feel like worship when she sang alone on this hill. Yet, each time she sang there, she would hear a negative voice inside her head. "Who are you to think anyone wants to hear what you have to offer? Do you think you're something special? What makes you think that?" the voice said. And for years and years, she'd let that voice rule her life. She simply wasn't worthy. But God had taught her to listen to another voice, a much softer voice, but insistent.

"Open your presents," it said. "I gave you gifts so you could use them."

Once upon a time, that would have made her laugh. Gifts? She had no gifts. But when she'd been stripped down to nothing, lying in a dark pit, God had reached down to her and His voice was like a rope she could cling to. She had grabbed on and held to it tightly. And she found that she did have some gifts. And one of them was to sing.

'Tis Grace that brought me safe thus far
And Grace will lead me home.

She finished that verse, the notes infused with a sense of longing and anticipation. And then they trailed away, echoing off the rocky hillsides in the distance. The houses in the windows below were closed to the evening chill, so she knew she wouldn't be bothering anybody. It was just her and God up here.

Or so she thought.

Behind her, someone cleared his throat.

She whirled around to see a man in a jogging suit standing by the twin pine trees. His face was red from exertion and cold. He was smiling at her.

"That was one of the most beautiful things I've ever heard," he said.

She felt herself blushing. Part of her wanted to run away and never look back. Someone had discovered her little act of worship and it was almost like he had opened the door to her bedroom. But the man's smile seemed genuine and he had said something nice to her.

"Thank you," she said softly, looking down at the brown grass beneath her feet.

"I hope I didn't scare you," he said. "It's just that I heard you when I was running down the forest trail and I couldn't help but come over and listen. Your voice is stunning. I've never heard that song sung better, and that's saying a lot."

"It's nothing," she mumbled. "I just like to come up here sometimes. . . ."

She again fought off the urge to run down the hill and back to her house. Instead, she shuffled her feet and put her hands behind her back.

"Did you ever sing professionally?" the man asked.

She looked up in surprise. Professionally? As in getting paid? She tried to answer, but only managed a confused grunt.

The man chuckled. "I want you to look at something," he said. He pointed down the hill. "See that large steeple there, next to the high school? That's my church. I'm an Elder there."

She nodded her head. She was familiar with that church. She'd never been inside it, but sometimes on Sunday mornings, when she'd been up here on her hill, she could hear music wafting out of the open windows. The music was heavenly, with the sound of choirs, and drums, and violins, and flutes. It always made her think of the Bible verse, "Make a joyful noise unto the Lord." Often she'd stop her own singing to listen to it and doing so felt like another act of worship, even from afar.

The man continued. "This is a crazy idea, and I'll have to run it by the Music Director, but I'd like you to come and sing for us this Sunday morning. It's a little different than what we usually do, but I think the contrast would be terrific – one solo voice in that huge church. You'd bring the house down."

She felt butterflies in her stomach. She'd never planned to sing in front of anyone - except for God, that is. And that other, bad voice had suddenly resurfaced. "They'll hate it," the voice said. "The music in a church like that is much too good for someone like you. Maybe they'll even laugh at you."

"I think you have a real gift," the man said, drowning out the bad voice momentarily. "And I should tell you, an awful lot of influential people go to my church, people who could do something for you." He rattled off the names of several Christian music artists who had gotten their start singing in his church. She knew some of the names. And he had said the word gift, so he was getting through to her.

"Wouldn't I have to practice or something?" she asked.

"Not for an *a capella* piece," he answered. "We'll set up a microphone for you and you can just come up and sing, like you did just now. 'Amazing Grace.' It'll be great. We'll all be incredibly blessed."

"I don't know . . ." she mumbled.

He frowned for a moment and reached into his pocket. "I can tell you're shy. Maybe you need some time to think it over. Here's my card. I'd love to have you do this. Call me by Friday so we can get your name in the bulletin. Trust me. You'll bring the house down." He put both hands on her shoulders and looked into her eyes. His face was sincere. "God has blessed you," he said. "And through you, He blessed me. Maybe there's a reason I went out running this evening."

He took off into the woods and left her standing there with his card in her hand. She looked down at the town and the church steeple in the distance. She felt her stomach churning like a washing machine. And her mind was a jumble. Whatever she decided to do or not do on Sunday morning, her own worship was over for this evening.

****

When Sunday morning came, she rolled out of bed an hour early. She hadn't slept much, for she'd decided to take the Elder up on his offer. All night long she'd been running the words to the song over and over in her head. Even though she'd sung it a thousand times, she had a terrible fear that she'd forget the words in front of all those people.

The bad voice inside her head kept tormenting her with one disaster scenario after another. "Maybe you'll fall down," it said. "Maybe your vocal cords will freeze up all together and you won't even be able to whisper. You've heard of things like that happening."

But she knew she had a gift. God had encouraged her to use it. And so had the Elder from the church. So she ignored the bad voice and got herself ready for church.

She'd planned to arrive at the church an hour early as the Elder had instructed her to do. But on this, of all days, her car wouldn't start. Of course she panicked and tried to figure out what to do. She paced around her driveway. Should she call the Elder to come and pick her up? No, he would be much too busy. And she didn't have any friends.

Finally, she decided to walk to church. It was about four miles distant, but she knew she could make it in time. She jogged, sprinted, and walked her way down long blocks, looking at her watch and trying to hurry as much as her wheezing breaths would allow. She came around the corner to the church just as the bell was ringing, announcing the beginning of the service.

She raced up the steps, the bad voice practically yelling now. "Look at all of these elegant people. What makes you think you can sing for them? They'll hate it. And besides, you're late!"

The Elder met her just inside the door. Instead of the relaxed, friendly face she had seen on the hill, he looked frazzled. "What took you?" he asked, wringing his hands.

She mumbled a few words about car trouble and when he noticed her frizzled hair and sweat-stained dress, he softened. "Okay," he whispered over the sound of organ music. "Glad you made it. But we run a pretty tight ship here. You're on right after the Explanatory Note. It'll be a good fit."

And then he hustled her into a pew near the front of the huge Sanctuary and sat her down. She turned to ask him a few questions, but he was already gone, nearly jogging down the aisle.

She looked around in panic, but suddenly everyone was standing up, so she stood up, too. The Music Team began playing from a stage at the front of the church. There was a full band, a brass section, violins, and even a penny whistle. Ten vocalists sang some of the most beautiful harmonies she had ever heard. Song lyrics were projected on a huge multimedia screen and the entire congregation sang along, raising their hands. She did love music, and it was hard not to love this. After a few verses of what turned out to be a very long medley, she found herself singing along. By the end of it, she was feeling just a little relaxed, like maybe she was a small part of this congregation. Everyone was focusing on the front of the church and on the music. They weren't looking at her. Was this what Heaven would be like someday, with everyone worshiping together?

But then the bad voice came back.

"Don't forget. You have to go up there soon. All by yourself. You're not ready for this."

She glanced all around the stage area. There were microphones everywhere. Which one was she supposed to use? And then her insides seemed to seize up all at once as a question filled her head. "When? When do I go up there?" She racked her brain. *What had the Elder said? After the Explanation Section? No that wasn't it. After the Expository? Something like that.*

She looked down at the pew. There had to be a bulletin so she could follow along and figure it out. The singing of those around her now fell off her like rain as she ran her hands over Bibles and hymnals in the backs of pews. No bulletins. She remembered seeing a stack of papers just inside the front door as she had come in. Did she have time to go back there and look? What if her song was coming up right after this one?

She felt paralyzed. She didn't want to make a mistake. She didn't want to let the Elder down. It sounded like he had gone out on a limb to get her here.

In a panic, she pushed through the standing people in her row and made her way back down the aisle. Maybe there would be enough time. She went over to the stack of papers. They were invitations to help serve at a homeless shelter. There was a box that was labeled "Bulletins." It was empty.

She made her way back to her pew just as the music was finishing up and everyone was sitting back down. She took a deep breath and tried, again, to remember. The Elder had said she was going to be doing a solo after something else during the service. Even if she didn't remember the name of the something else, if she watched closely, she should be able to figure it out. She could just walk up there and do her song. And then it would all be over.

The Elder had not been joking when he said the church ran a pretty tight ship. One thing flowed into another in rapid succession. There were testimonials, video presentations, more music, and prayers on the screen that everyone followed along with. The pastor gave a tightly scripted sermon. She tried to pay attention, but she was simply too nervous.

"You should forget the whole thing," said the bad voice inside her head. "You're not ready. You'll never be ready."

"Stop it!" she shouted, not audibly, but deep inside, and the voice got quieter . . . though it never went completely away.

After the sermon came the offering, accompanied by more music, this time subdued but beautiful, with a lot of humming. And then came something else. The Pastor was reading off notes. Was this it? It had to be. She must be on next.

She looked down at her folded, ice cold hands. She began running the words to "Amazing Grace" through her head, humming almost inaudibly, squeezing her eyes shut. It felt like she were standing at the edge of a cliff, but she was ready. She wouldn't mess this up.

In her concentration, she didn't notice that the Pastor had stopped reading. There was a pause in the church for maybe thirty seconds. She looked up. Someone had set a single microphone on a stand at the front of the altar. A bright white light was shining down on it from high above. The Music Team was looking around as if something was wrong.

She felt her legs turn to rubber. This was it! They were waiting for her! She slowly got to her feet, her knees shaking, and began to push her way out of the pew. The aisle suddenly seemed like miles away.

The Music Director turned toward his team and waved his hand. They began another song. It wasn't "Amazing Grace." The white light from above was turned off and someone came and took the microphone stand away. Just like that.

She stood there for a moment, swaying on her feet with her mouth open. Everyone around her stood up and began singing the closing hymn.

She put her hand up as if to stop everything. She wanted to sing her song, she really did. But they'd already passed her by.

The closing hymn was a blur to her, and when everyone

walked back down the aisle to leave, she was carried along like flotsam. She shook the Pastor's hand like everyone else, and staggered toward the open church doors. A hand caught her shoulder. She spun around. It was the Elder.

"Did you get cold feet?" he asked. His face didn't look angry.

"N . . . no," she said. "I was getting ready to come up there but. . . ."

"I know," he said, like a kindly father to his daughter. "I never should have asked you. You just aren't ready for something like this. Maybe down the road."

He hugged her and said, "I hope you'll come back to our church next week. We have a singer coming in that I know you'll love. She's got a new album coming out next month. I think she could be an inspiration to you."

And with that, he left her standing in the entranceway.

****

It took her a long time to recover. She wondered if she'd ever completely get past what had happened to her at the church. Maybe in the great scheme of things it wasn't much, just a missed song. But several months later she was still waking up in the middle of the night, reliving the awful scene in the pew, when she had tried to go up there but they had just moved on without her. It was like one of those dreams where you try to run but your legs won't move.

She had prayed about it many times, looking for answers. Why had God allowed that to happen to her, when all she had wanted to do was to use her gifts to worship

Him? The only good thing was that the bad voice had been blessedly silent. Maybe it knew it had already done enough damage for awhile. And deep inside, she still knew she could sing.

It was a Sunday morning when she decided to finally return to her hill. All the way up there, she felt emotion welling up. As she got to the twin pine trees, she sat down in the brown grass and hugged her knees. Tears came to her eyes, slowly at first and then in a torrent. It was the first time she had cried since that morning in the church. Her body shook as she sobbed, cleansing all the bad thoughts from her head and her heart. She wept for a full ten minutes.

When she finally got shakily to her feet, she heard muffled music coming from the church in the distance. It sounded professional. And somehow, after getting all the grief out of her system, it didn't make her feel bad.

Would she ever try again? she wondered. *To sing for other people, that is? Maybe.*

But in the meantime, she knew what she had to do. In counterpoint to the professional music coming from the church in the distance, she opened her mouth and began to sing, almost whispering at first, and then building to a crescendo at the end.

> *We've no less days to sing God's praise*
> *Than when we've first begun.*

It was an act of worship.

PARABLE 8:
THE CAVES

They were the People of the Caves. They went about their business during the day, when ambient light radiated from the walls because of … well, no one knew what caused the walls to glow. Some people said that the light filtered through from the Outside, but most people didn't believe there was an Outside. Scientists had several theories to explain the light, but when it came right down to it, no one knew for sure. And to really think there was anything outside of the Caves was … well, considered childish.

Since time began, people had dwelled in the Caves. They grew crops in the caverns where the walls glowed brightest. They domesticated animals. And they tried to live their lives as best as they could, playing games, feasting, singing songs, and telling stories.

At the end of each day, the walls grew dim. It was then that the people rested and slept and dreamed dreams.

The Dreamer was more imaginative than most boys his age. He would constantly ask his father questions.

"What are we here for?" he asked him one evening before bed.

"That one's easy," his father said. "We're here to treat each other with love, because that's what the One Who Went Before tells us to do."

The Dreamer had heard this before, because his father was one of the Believers. There was an oft-told story about a man who had come to the Caves from the Outside. Some said he was sent by the Maker of the Caves. Some said he actually was the Maker. And he came to show the people the way to the Outside, a beautiful place where, when you looked up, you didn't see dark rock, but an infinite expanse of blue and white.

"You need to understand," the boy's father said, "that the Maker loves us so much that he left his perfect world to come here to be one of us, to show us how to live with each other. And he lived his life here, and he died. The Side Passage appeared to him the way it eventually does for all people. But he went through it to the Outside, and then came back, just for a short while, to leave his spirit behind to show us the way."

"But how can you know that, when you can't even see him?" asked The Dreamer.

"Here," his father said. "This is the story of The One Who Went Before. It will answer all your questions." He handed him a bulky book with a worn leather cover.

That night, as he was lying in bed in the dim light from the walls, The Dreamer began to read. The book was hard to understand at first, and not nearly as exciting as the adventure books he usually read, so he set it aside. But he was sure he believed in The One Who Went Before, because his father told him it was true.

But eventually, The Dreamer reached an age where most young people separate themselves from their parents' ideas. His teachers and friends began to tell him other things. They said that the Believers were only chasing after fairy tales. Of course it would be nice if there were an Outside, they said, but wishing for it didn't make it so. The Caves were all there was, and any intelligent person knew that. Eventually, they convinced The Dreamer and he no longer believed.

When he told his father, he was hurt, of course. But he gave him a rueful smile and said, "Someday you'll need to believe. And then the Spirit of the One Who Went Before will find you."

The Dreamer went on with his life. He met a girl and married. He had children of his own and moved to his own cavern. He prospered. But still he kept in touch with his father, and cherished the times they got to spend together, taking long walks through the caverns just before it got dark.

They met so often that The Dreamer never even noticed the changes that were gradually taking place in his father. He hardly noticed his steps slowing down, nor his face becoming wrinkled. He was still just his father, someone who had always been there for him and always would be.

So it was a terrible shock when, one day during their walk, his father pulled up short. The Dreamer kept on for a couple of steps until he noticed that his father wasn't alongside. He turned back around and saw him waiting there, looking into his face.

"What is it?" The Dreamer asked, alarmed.

His father didn't reply, but tipped his head slightly, toward the wall to his right. Instead of solid rock, a dark passage had appeared where there had been none before. The Dreamer knew what that passage meant, for he had seen his grandfather go down one like it a long time ago. And as with anyone else who had made that journey, his grandfather had never returned.

"No!" was all The Dreamer managed to say.

His father looked at him with an expression that could only be described as joy, mixed with compassion. "Don't be sad," he said. "This is not the end. The One Who Came Before has marked the way through. The Caves are not all there is, not even close. They're just the beginning. There is an Outside. I know that with every fiber of my being. This passage will take me there. And you can go there, too – when your time comes. And all you have to do is believe." And then he turned away.

"Wait!" shouted The Dreamer, but his father was already walking down the dark passageway, head held high. The Dreamer tried to follow, but the opening had already closed up, leaving him to stare through his tears at the solid rock.

✳✳✳✳

Many years passed. The Dreamer's grief over the loss of his father eased somewhat, although he was never completely gone from his thoughts. Like all the other People of the Caves, he worked and played and loved. He raised his children and remained faithful to his wife. But always, he wrestled with the old questions.

Was there an Outside? If, when people took the Side Passage, they were really just passing to the Outside, why didn't some of them come back to let others know it was there? Or was his father's book right that only one had ever done that?

His father's book. The Dreamer tried to read it a little more often as he got older. It brought him a small measure of comfort during bad times, even if he didn't believe it. And sometimes. . . .

There was one verse in that book that always seemed to stay with him. And it was that verse that came to him on the last evening of his life. He was walking toward his cavern after a long day of work, when he felt a sharp stab of pain in his chest. At that moment, the words of that verse flooded into his head: "For God so loved the world, that He gave His only begotten Son, that whoever believes in Him shall not perish, but have eternal life."

Believe. That's what his father had asked him to do. Eternal life. That meant that he wouldn't die, but would go on. Go on where? To the Outside, of course. Suddenly, it all seemed to make sense.

As the pain in his chest increased, a Passage opened in the rock to his right. The fear that had been welling up in him eased, even though he knew what was happening, and he'd dreaded this moment nearly his entire life. Yes, the Passage was dark. And yes, it represented the unknown. Anyone would be afraid of that. But the words of the book said that this wasn't the end. And now he finally believed.

The Dreamer staggered toward the opening, still clutching his chest. He went through it. The wall closed behind him. Immediately, the Passage began to glow, with a kind of light his eyes had never seen, a clear, bright, vibrant light, not like the subdued, diffused light he had lived in all his life. And the light was coming from in front of him. The pain in his chest disappeared as fast as it had come on. He moved forward down the passage and toward the light, nearly running now. He never thought of looking back, not even once.

Finally, with one triumphant step, he broke free of the passageway. He was no longer in the Caves. He found himself standing in a vast, open space, gaping up at an endless expanse of blue above his head, flecked with soft, white, cottony shapes. A gentle breeze caressed his face. The light was brilliant, but somehow it didn't make him squint. It was the most stunningly beautiful thing he had ever seen.

And in that moment, The Dreamer understood why people did not return to the Caves after they made it here. That would be like trying to go back into your mother's womb after you were born. And it truly felt to The Dreamer like he had just been born, again.

Now, another quote from the book came into his head. It seemed appropriate, considering the circumstances. It was a direct quote from The One Who Went Before. "I am the Light of the world," He had said. "He who follows Me will not walk in the darkness, but will have the Light of life."

The Dreamer didn't even look back as he walked from the darkness into that light, and then set out to find his loved ones who had gone before.

PARABLE 9:
THE VALLEY

"This is the best place on Earth," I said, taking a deep breath of the pine-scented air. Birds flitted from the tops of the majestic trees that surrounded me. Through the branches, I could see the bluer-than-blue sky. Off to my right, a brook cascaded over pebbles. Deer and elk pranced through a meadow in the distance and squirrels chattered among the acorns at my feet.

"I finally made it," I said. "The top of the mountain."

I knew I'd never have to leave this place. I'd worked so very hard to get here, grunting and sweating for who knows how long, my legs ready to give out at any moment on the long, long climb. But just this morning I'd crested the top. The feeling of relief and joy that were flooding through me were worth all the effort.

"God, I love it here," I said.

"I know you do," said a soft voice from behind me.

I whirled around to see The Teacher smiling at me with eyes like stars. I rushed forward and threw my arms around Him. He held me in His embrace for a long moment until I pulled away.

"You made a beautiful place," I said.

"Thanks," He said, laughing.

"I mean, the meadows and the mountain peaks in the distance. And the skies. How can they be so blue? And the animals aren't even afraid of me. . . ." I went on and on like this for several minutes.

"So, you like it here," He said after I had finally wound down.

Chuckling, I said, "I can't believe I really made it . . . after all that time. I guess I'm pretty proud of myself."

"You should be," He replied. "I'm pleased with you too. You never gave up."

I felt my chest swell. "I'm not ashamed to admit that I wanted to quit. A bunch of times."

He nodded.

"That's why it feels so good to be here. I deserve it."

"Of course you do," He answered.

"And you want me to enjoy this."

"Of course."

There had been no hesitation in His voice, no questioning. So why did I suddenly feel so uneasy?

"Come," He said, "I'll show you around. Let's take a walk in the meadow."

We left the forest and strolled among a field of wildflowers. We came to a pond, sitting down to rest on a rough-hewn, wooden bench at the edge of the water. The Teacher filled His flask with crystal clear water from a spring feeding the pond. Then He retrieved some bread from a pocket in His robe. We shared the simple meal. The bread tasted freshly baked, though how it could be so I couldn't say. And the water. The water tasted better than the finest wine I had ever sipped when I had lived in the valley.

"Is there something wrong?" He asked. "You've been quiet since we left the forest."

"I don't know," I said, "I'm just feeling uneasy. Maybe I don't know what to do with myself, now that I'm finally here."

He smiled. "That's the way of things, isn't it? We strive for so long to get somewhere that when we finally make it . . . well. . . ."

When we had finished the bread, The Teacher got to his feet and put the flask back inside His pocket. "Follow me," He said.

We walked to the end of the meadow and onto a rocky path. As the path wound gradually around the peak, the wildflowers faded away, until there were only boulders everywhere. At the end of the path was another bench. He sat down and motioned for me to sit beside Him. When I did, I glanced down and gasped. We were on the edge of a huge outcropping. Far, far below us I could see the path I had followed to the top of the mountain. I traced its winding contours and switchbacks all the way down to the bottom, just at the edge of my vision.

"Is that where I came from?" I asked.

He nodded. "That's The Valley, the place you worked so hard to get out of."

Even from this distance, The Valley was a seething, swirling, snake pit. People were running frantically to and fro, clutching and grabbing, fighting and clawing, even killing each other. They were barely visible through an ugly carpet of greenish-brown smog.

"It's like a cesspool down there," I said, dragging my eyes away and returning them to the bluer-than-blue sky above.

"Yes it is," He said, rather solemnly, I thought.

My uneasiness returned and I felt butterflies in my stomach. "Why did You bring me out to this ledge?" I asked, holding tightly to the bench while gazing down at the scene below.

"Because I want you to remember," He said.

"Remember what?" I asked.

"Where you came from."

"Oh, I'll never forget that," I said. "Why do you think I'm so glad to be up here?"

"More than that," He said.

"What?"

He paused a moment. "Do you remember that day when you were about halfway up the mountain, the day when it wouldn't stop raining?"

I grimaced. How could I ever forget? It was like getting caught in a monsoon. Desperately searching for a little bit of shelter, I was walking across a narrow ledge when suddenly great sheets of water were running down the mountain all around me, stopping me in my tracks. I was sure I'd be washed off the ledge and smashed onto the rocks a thousand feet below. But it was the strangest thing. The water crashed down behind me and in front of me, but the place where I was standing stayed dry.

"There must have been a large rock somewhere above the ledge, deflecting the water away from me," I said.

"There was," He said.

I looked into his eyes. Chills ran up my spine as I absorbed the meaning of what He had just said.

"Remember that night in the snow?" He continued.

I shuddered. That had been as dark and frigid a night as I'd ever experienced in my life. My teeth wouldn't stop chattering and my feeble blanket might as well have been made out of rice paper. I was sure I was going to freeze to death. In the middle of the night I got up and began stuffing things into my backpack, ready to give up and go back down into The Valley, for as bad it was down there, at least it would be warmer. But then suddenly the wind had changed direction and things began to thaw. It was eerie, but that had changed my mind about giving up.

"It was almost like someone lit a fire nearby," I mumbled.

"Someone did," answered The Teacher.

Another chill ran up my spine as I struggled to absorb that one.

"Remember the time you tripped as you were going across the boulder field?" He asked.

I gritted my teeth. That had been the worst moment of all. I should have died for sure. I found myself sliding down the mountain with an avalanche of stones all around me, my arms pin wheeling. At the last possible moment my hand found a branch, maybe an ancient tree root. I clutched it with both hands and it stopped my fall. In my wild rush of panic and adrenaline, it almost felt like someone was pulling on the other end as I scrambled up to safety. But I was alone on that. . . .

I gaped at The Teacher. "You were on the other end of that stick?" I asked.

He looked at me with shining eyes. "What man is there among you who has a sheep, and if it falls into a pit on the Sabbath, will he not take hold of it and lift it out?"

My face flushed with shame. I had been so proud of myself. "So You were there the whole way," I said, softly.

"Lo, I am with you always," He replied.

His words didn't comfort me like they should have. I had thought all along that it was my own striving that had gotten me here. Now I hung my head.

He put His hand on my shoulder. "I'm proud of you," He said. "And it's right for you to be proud of yourself. That was a long, long climb. And you never gave up, even though you wanted to."

"But I thought. . . ."

"Hush," He said. "Let's just enjoy the view."

We sat there looking at the sky and the distant, snowy peaks. An eagle swooped low and glided gracefully away on the breeze. I tried my best not to look down, but finally, I couldn't help myself. And what I saw made my stomach churn.

"The Valley is such a wretched place," I muttered.

"It's a needy place," He said.

I pulled away from Him. I knew what was coming next.

"No!" I shouted. "I can't do it. I won't do it!" I felt tears of frustration come to my eyes.

"But I didn't say anything," He said.

"I know what You're going to ask. You're going to ask me to go back down there, aren't You?"

"Only if you want to," He said.

"But . . . why? It's hopeless." I pointed my finger down at The Valley. "Look at them. Most of them don't even want to be rescued. They like it down there!"

The Teacher's eyes flashed. "Did you like it down there?"

"Of course I didn't like it. Why do you think I came up here? I'm not like them. I'm better than they are!"

The words had slipped out of my mouth before I'd had time to think. Now they echoed down into the Valley and onto the heads of the people I had just passed judgment upon.

The Teacher patted my hand. "You need some time," He said gracefully. "I'm really glad you're here."

There had been no anger in His voice, no disappointment. But as He stood to leave, all the anger that I had been aiming at Him suddenly turned back upon myself.

* * * *

I endured some sleepless nights after that. But in the daytime, I was free to explore the mountaintop. Everywhere I went the beauty was simply stunning. I had time to do all the things I'd always wanted to do – I built a cabin, I wrote books, I hiked and fished, I camped out in the woods. But increasingly, I found myself drawn to the rocky path that led up to the outcropping.

One day, against my better judgment, I again climbed that path. I sat alone on the bench and gazed down upon The Valley. Nothing had changed. But as I sat there, I began to remember what it had been like to live down there. So many feelings came back to me, feelings that had faded away while I had been living on the mountaintop. I remembered the helplessness and despair, and most of all, the bitterness I'd felt toward those who didn't have to live in the Valley. I also remembered my disappointment at those who had refused to come with me when I started my climb to the top, even though I had begged them to come along. Why hadn't they joined me? Didn't they know there was something better?

I came back to that outcropping the next day as well, and the day after that. And each time I stayed a little bit longer.

****

On a crisp morning in the fall, I left my cabin and found myself on the path that led down off the mountain. I took a deep breath of the cool, sweet alpine air, wishing I could keep it in my lungs forever. But I knew that I couldn't. Where I was going, the air would not be sweet at all.

I had gotten a vision. In my mind, I was leading a group of people out of The Valley. It wasn't a large group, because I certainly couldn't help them all. But I could help some. I would help anyone who wanted to leave that place. I could tell them that I had been to the mountaintop and I knew how beautiful it was. And if I stumbled, maybe The Teacher would help me again. Maybe He would help us.

How long would I be away from the mountaintop? Maybe forever. But I felt like I was prepared for that. For just like long ago, when I had first set out to leave The Valley, I knew I had to at least try.

I knelt down and took one last drink of clear, icy water from the spring. I whispered a soft prayer that if and when I finally did make it back up here, I wouldn't be alone.

PARABLE 10:
THE DARKNESS

I found myself in a very dark place. It was some sort of tunnel, or cavern, a place where light could only shine briefly, if at all. I ran my hands along the rough stone walls as I groped my way down a passageway. I tested the ground with my feet, hoping I would feel a drop-off or a hole before I stepped blindly into it.

The Lord was with me. I felt Him there in the overwhelming blackness.

"Lord, get me out of here," I mumbled through clenched teeth.

"I am here with you," He said.

"I don't know the way out of here," I said, appalled at how weak and terrified my own voice sounded.

"I am right next to you," He answered.

"But what do I do? Which way do I go? There are so many passageways that cross this one. I could be lost in here forever."

"I will stay with you forever," He said. "I will never leave you or forsake you."

As the Lord spoke, a faint light glimmered ahead, only for the briefest of moments. I saw a junction, and the light flickered down the pathway to the right.

"Do I go that way, Lord?"

He did not answer, but I felt Him still there beside me. I groped my way ahead, and when I came to the junction, I went to the right.

"Why can't you just get me out of here?" I pleaded.

He put His hand upon my shoulder and it felt strong and reassuring. But the passageway was completely dark again and I trembled.

"Lo, I am with you always," He said.

"But it's so dark. Why can't You just pick me up and carry me out of here?"

His hand tightened on my shoulder and He steered me gently over to the other side of the passageway. My left hand found the opposite wall and I moved ahead. Dim light flickered briefly and I saw something off to my right, a gaping pit. I moved past it as the light blinked out again.

"If you find yourself here again, you will know the way past it safely," the Lord whispered, His words echoing off the stone and clinging dirt.

I stopped in my tracks. My knees shook and I felt dizzy. I thought about the pit behind me. I might have stepped into it. How deep was it? Would I have fallen into space, falling and falling, my arms pin wheeling? Would I have crashed into the bottom like a rag doll, smashing my bones into little pieces? How many more pits were up ahead, and would I be able to avoid them all?

"I can't go on," I cried. Then I crumbled to the ground. "It's too dangerous here."

"But you have to go on," He said.

"Carry me," I said.

"I am with you."

I shook my head. Frustration and anger began to burn inside of me. "You keep saying that," I said. "But what good does it do me? You could get me out of here in a heartbeat, I know You could. I should just send You away for all the help You're giving me. You don't understand how bad this feels, how scared I am!"

I hugged my knees tight to my chest and my breath came in ragged gasps. I wanted to cry but the tears wouldn't come. I sat like that for a long time, shaking.

It was deathly quiet in the darkness.

"Lord?" I said, and my words bounced back at me from the stone walls. There was no answer.

Now I felt real panic. Anything I'd felt before was nothing compared to this. Now I was really alone, adrift in a sea of blackness. What had I done? My heart raced and skipped in my chest and my unseeing eyes darted back and forth.

I heard a sound. I listened for a moment and the sound became clearer. The Lord was sitting next to me in the darkness, weeping.

"Lord?" I said.

"I am with you," He answered in a husky voice.

Moments ago those words had made me angry. Now they sounded like the music of Heaven.

"I'm so sorry, Lord. I didn't mean what I said."

"My God, My God. Why have You forsaken Me?" He said.

"What?" I asked.

"I said that once," He answered.

"Yes, You did," I said, and remembered the words. I had read them many times, but had never really felt them in my heart before.

"You need to understand something," said the Lord. "I know darkness. I felt it many times. I spent a long, dark night on My knees in Gethsemane. All My friends deserted Me and went to sleep. I knew that the soldiers would come for Me soon. I wondered if I would be able to stand up to what was coming. Would I be able to bear the shame and humiliation? Would I be able to be strong when people spit on Me, beat Me, and drove nails through My hands? I asked that the cup be taken from Me. I asked My Father to carry Me away from the darkness and into the light. But He left Me there in the garden and the soldiers came."

As the Lord spoke, I stopped shaking. His words cut through my fear like a scythe through wheat. I felt closer to the Lord than I had ever been, as we sat there in the dark.

"This reminds me of something," I said. "When I was a kid, my friend and I decided to turn out all the lights in his basement so we could crawl around in the dark. It's just the kind of thing kids do, I guess. We shuffled around on our hands and knees for awhile, scared stiff. I wandered off behind the big, growling furnace, away from my friend. I knew he was out there somewhere, but I didn't know where. I was terrified, and I almost hollered to my friend to go turn on the lights. But I kept going, kept wandering around, until my friend bumped into me in the dark. We both laughed with relief and I knew then that he had been scared, too. Somehow that made me feel a lot better. I was still scared, but I wasn't alone."

"I understand," said the Lord, and I knew then that He did. And I finally realized why He had endured so much, given up so much, and suffered so much to become one of us. It was for times like these.

There were a few moments more of silence as I pondered all of that in the darkness. Then the Lord spoke. "So what will you do now?" He asked.

I had been wondering about that myself. And there seemed to be only one answer. "I suppose we ought to get moving," I said. "Maybe the way out is up ahead."

"Maybe it is," answered the Lord.

He stood up in the blackness and I sensed Him there, reaching down His hand to me. I reached up and grabbed it. It felt warm and solid. He pulled me to my feet.

With my other hand I found the stone wall to my left. I began to inch slowly forward, always keeping one hand on that wall and the other on the Lord. In the pitch black darkness, I hoped to somehow avoid the dark pits that were surely waiting for me. But I wasn't alone.

And in that way, the two of us moved forward together through the overwhelming darkness, toward what I hoped would be the healing light of day.

PARABLE 11:
THE CHURCH

It was called simply "The Church," a huge understatement. It took up one whole block of downtown and boasted offices for all its employees, meeting halls, teaching classrooms, and parking for a thousand cars. It had a coffee shop that made Starbucks look like somebody's kitchen. There was a bookstore featuring Christian best-sellers and a wide variety of inspirational plaques, CD's, posters for your wall, and one whole section with an archive of every sermon The Pastor had given since he first opened The Church's doors.

All of this was impressive enough to the casual visitor, but it was the Sanctuary itself that took your breath away, for it was an architectural masterpiece. You could see its tapering crystal tower from blocks away. As you walked closer, it resembled a huge, shining diamond, its thousands of facets reflecting the sunlight upward, always upward. At night, spotlights tucked inside each and every facet made the Sanctuary glow from within, a beacon for all to see. And lots of people followed that beacon. The polished wooden pews were usually full on Sunday mornings and evenings, Saturday nights, and on Mondays and Wednesdays for Bible study and meditation.

But what The Pastor liked best was the fact that the Church was as spotless and pure as a white choir robe. Every square inch of floor shone like a new penny. The entire inside was freshly painted three times a year. If somebody made even a tiny scratch in a single pew, a staff member came along and rubbed it until the scratch was gone, or the pew was replaced. Whenever he gave communion, The Pastor could see his reflection in the cups and plates. The kneeling cushions were covered in expensive fabric that was laundered every Monday morning. The pulpit was made of flawless Travertine limestone, imported from Italy. Even the cross, which was fastened high up on one of the crystal facets, was made of two pieces of mahogany, specially selected for the matching lines of their wood grain, and kept dust free with a special piece of cambric linen attached to a long pole.

Yes, it was more than just a church. It was a true showplace to rival the cathedrals dotting the landscapes of Europe, built a thousand years ago by people whose religion had been an integral part of their daily lives. Those cathedrals were now just relics, full of moss and cracks in the stone, just like the religion of the people that had once built them. But this was America and The Church was very much alive.

It was the thing in world The Pastor was most proud of, especially considering that the whole thing had started with just a simple storefront church in the city. It was his monument to God, Who had plucked him from his old life of selfishness and put him on a shining path.

Or so he thought.

****

He would never have been a pastor in the first place if God hadn't intervened in his life. At least he thought it was God. Or maybe he was just tired. In those days, he was just a law student, struggling to get through school.

He shouldn't have tried to drive home that night. He'd been at the library studying for finals and he'd been going on very little sleep for weeks. But he wanted to get home to his own bed. He had only made it four blocks before he fell asleep at the wheel and crashed into a utility pole. His clunker of a car was too old for air bags so his head hit the windshield and he fractured his skull. He should have died, but thanks to some very skillful surgeons and the state's medical plan for indigents, he pulled through. Even so, he was in the hospital for months and his career plans were put on hold.

One day an elderly man came into his hospital room. The student had never seen the man before.

"How ya' doin'?" the man asked as he shook the student's hand. "They call me The Shepherd around here.

Looks like you could use some company."

He was wearing a clerical collar so the student assumed he was the hospital chaplain. And the man was right about him needing company, for he had no family left alive and the few acquaintances he'd made in law school had long since grown tired of coming to visit.

"Mind if I pull up a chair?" asked The Shepherd.

"Suit yourself," mumbled the student.

They exchanged some pleasantries for a while until The Shepherd said softly, "Tell me about yourself."

The student supposed he should have clammed up. He didn't know this man from Adam. But he'd been lying in a hospital bed for a long time. So he told the man his whole life story. He told him how he was working to escape the agonizing poverty that had destroyed his family when he was growing up. He told him how he was putting himself through law school to change all of that, and how he planned to become very rich. But now all of that was in doubt.

The Shepherd reached over and touched his hand beneath the sheet. "Sounds like you've had a rough go of it," he said.

Something about his manner made the student feel like The Shepherd really did understand. "I guess so," he mumbled.

"So now that you're getting better," The Shepherd said, "what are you planning to do with the rest of your life? Are you going back to law school?"

The student had been thinking about that a lot lately. "At first I thought I would," he said, "but now I'm not so sure."

The Shepherd chuckled. "It's amazing what a few months in bed will do to our dreams." He stood up and stretched. "Do you mind if I tell you something?" He was looking down at the student in the bed, looking right into his eyes. For some reason it was making the young man squirm.

"What?" the student asked quietly.

"You speak very well," The Shepherd said.

"Speak?"

"Yes. The way you put sentences together, and the way you just told me about your life, I found it very gripping. You have a gift. They used to call it the 'gift of gab.' A gift like that can change people's lives. Especially yours."

The student felt his face grow hot. He hadn't been expecting this. "Thanks, I think," he managed to say.

"You should take advantage of that gift," The Shepherd said. "There are good places to use it other than in court-rooms."

"Like where?"

"Oh, that's for you to figure out."

The Shepherd winked and left the room. Just like that.

The student looked down. Several small, brightly colored pamphlets were scattered on his bed, evidently dropped there by The Shepherd. And on his bed stand was a Bible.

So he started reading. He no longer focused on law books, which he'd gotten very tired of, but on the Bible, which he'd never read before. Just a few weeks later, very late at night, he received his calling.

He was having trouble getting to sleep. He was gazing out the hospital window at the scene below. This was City Hospital, not in the best neighborhood, so there were drunks staggering by on the sidewalk. Glass bottles shattered against brick walls down the block. There was an empty lot across the street, with homeless people huddled around fires in old garbage cans. The scene brought back painful memories as the student remembered what it was like to be dirt poor. He didn't think he'd ever end up as poor as those wretches down there – even his parents hadn't made life choices that bad, but still it made him feel uneasy.

Suddenly, he received what he could only describe as a vision. First he heard a voice inside his head. It simply said, "There is my church."

He shook his head in confusion. Church? He didn't see any church, just an empty lot with a bunch of homeless people. But the longer he stared, the more his fertile mind began to work. Before long, he was seeing a gleaming cathedral instead of an empty lot. It had brilliant spotlights that pierced the smog-filled sky of the city like a beacon. It had a large set of double doors opening inwards.

Thousands of people were swarming inside towards a glowing light that radiated from within. As they went through the doors, their posture changed. They threw up their hands and collapsed to their knees. They were being transformed on the spot, all because of the cathedral.

No, that wasn't right. It wouldn't be called a cathedral. It would be called simply "The Church." And he would build it.

And that's when he knew he wasn't going back to law school.

****

It took him many, many years of hard work to realize his dream. He started with a simple storefront church, preaching every Sunday to the best of his ability. But it turned out that he really did have a gift of gab, as The Shepherd had called it. It didn't take long before his storefront church was outgrowing its space. He rented a bigger building and more people came. Eventually, that meeting place was bursting at the seams as well. And he seemed to be attracting all the right types of people – doctors, CEOs, pillars of the community, even lawyers. It was people like that who helped make his vision a reality. Because it takes a lot of money to build something like The Church.

Yes, there were less and less street people in the pews on Sundays. But that was okay. There are always plenty of places for them to go, places like his original storefront church. And his new, bigger church was thriving. He was able to buy the empty lot across from the hospital and start construction. A year later, The Sanctuary was finished and as The Pastor, he had started the first of many building programs. A staff was in place. His vision had become a reality.

But sometimes he would glance up toward the window of the room in the hospital across the street, where he had been standing when the vision came – a vision powerful enough to carry him forward to its fulfillment. He had succeeded, yet mixed with his pride over that, another feeling sometimes dogged him, usually late at night. Emptiness.

****

One early January, after a mild Christmas season, during which The Church had brought in a record amount of offerings, winter finally arrived in the city. It was cold in the streets, and snow whirled around like phantoms in the sub-zero temperatures. The Pastor was feeling restless, the way he usually did when Christmas was over. He decided to take a walk around the entire complex.

As he was passing the front entrance of City Hospital, suddenly he thought of the man who had come to his bedside that night. The man had said that everyone just called him "The Shepherd." Maybe he was still working at the hospital. He shouldn't be too hard to find. The Pastor had never gotten a chance to thank the man. And even though he was The Pastor and had counseled lots of people, on this cold, lonely night, he felt like he needed some advice for a change.

Ten minutes later he was scratching his head in confusion. The woman at the front desk of the hospital, who had been working at City Hospital for over twenty years, had never heard of a chaplain called "The Shepherd." And on the wall with pictures of all the chaplains from the past thirty years, there was no picture of him.

The Pastor felt a chill as he stood by that wall. Of course the man could have been an itinerant preacher that came to hospitals once in awhile to leave pamphlets. But somehow that didn't ring true.

But there was no time for The Pastor to reflect on the

116

mystery. For it was then that he heard the wail of sirens from outside the hospital doors and down the block. . . .

****

The investigators said it was faulty wiring in the heating system that had started the fire in The Church. Maybe it was because the furnace had been struggling mightily to heat such a massive space on such a cold January night. But whatever had caused it, the fire burned incredibly fast, and all The Pastor could do was watch, shivering in the cold as legions of fire trucks tried to put out the fast-moving flames. Some of the hi-tech plastics used in parts of the building had turned out to be extremely flammable and it was all over in minutes, just like in an Old Testament plague.

As news helicopters hovered overhead, The Pastor could only watch his shining dream crumble into a huge pile of ashes and blackened metal. When it was over, he felt more empty than he had ever felt in his life.

****

How do you get over something like that? How do you get past the fact that when you believed God was leading you, and He wanted you to do His work, that He destroyed it all in a single, frosty night, like a kid would destroy a tower of blocks? The Pastor's heart turned as black as the burnt wreckage that now covered the city block The Church complex had occupied. To make matters worse,

The Church CFO had made a fraudulent deal with the insurance company, so when the Church burned, he had run off with the kickback money, and there were no funds to rebuild. As a result, not only did The Pastor lose his church, he had also been betrayed by a trusted friend.

He tried to get his enthusiasm back. He sent e-mails to the entire congregation, telling them that he was going to rent space in a storefront a few blocks away and start all over again. But it was amazing how quickly they all found other places to worship. The Church hadn't been around long enough to establish deep roots. No one had kids who had grown up in The Church, with all the ties of loyalty that entails. And The Pastor guessed that he himself seemed much less impressive personally now, without an elegant showplace standing behind him.

So the whole organization came crashing down. There was still a lot of debt on the building, and without the insurance money to pay it off, The Church's finances were quickly in shambles. There was no money to pay employees. No money to pay The Pastor. He lost his house and his two BMWs. He retreated from the public, rented a cheap room in the city, and tried to figure out what he was going to do next. And he tried to pray. . . .

* * * *

Exactly one year later, the city was suffering through another cold spell. The Pastor was wrestling with his usual after-Christmas blues, worse than ever this year because of all that had happened. He had been working a series of part-time jobs. He never attended church, because that just stirred up memories of everything he'd lost.

Out walking at sunset, he found himself by the site of the old church. By now, it had reverted to the empty lot he had seen that night from the hospital, only the empty lot was larger, like the emptiness in his heart when he passed the site. The Pastor's hands were in his pockets and his head was down, his collar turned up against the icy wind, as he walked.

"Hi," said a voice behind him.

He whirled around to see The Shepherd.

The Pastor gaped at the man for a few moments. "What are you doing here?" he finally managed to blurt out.

"Looks like you could use some company," answered The Shepherd, repeating what he had said that night in the hospital.

The Pastor was speechless.

"Will you walk with me?" asked The Shepherd.

A lot of things raced through The Pastor's mind. He thought about telling The Shepherd what he had found out at the hospital. He thought about asking the man who he really was. But somehow it didn't seem to matter. He felt warmer just standing beside the man. And he had to admit it was good to see him again. So he fell into step beside him.

As they rounded the first corner, The Pastor blurted out, "You changed my life."

"I imagine by now you're thinking that wasn't such a good thing," answered The Shepherd.

The Pastor almost chuckled. "That's an understatement," he whispered.

"You thought you were following God," The Shepherd said.

The Pastor could only nod his head.

"And you feel like God pulled the rug out from under you, that He destroyed your gift to Him."

The Pastor nodded again.

By now it was fully dark, and the night air was even colder. The Pastor shivered.

"The Church was a beautiful place," continued The Shepherd. "It brought people in from all over the city to hear the gospel. Some people's lives were changed for the better, just like in your vision."

The Pastor thought about asking the man how He knew about that vision. Instead, he simply listened.

"You led some people to God. No one can deny that. And The Church was a great blessing to the city. But it wasn't about God."

The Pastor paused mid-stride and turned on him. "What do you mean it wasn't about God? I was following His will when I built it. It was my vision."

The Shepherd looked him in the eye and The Pastor felt himself squirm, just like that night in the hospital bed.

"Whose vision was it?" asked The Shepherd.

"My vision," The Pastor answered. "It was my. . . ."

And then The Pastor knew. It had all been about him. It was his house of cards, built incredibly high to show the world what a great man he was. That realization made him weep, as all the frustrations and grief of the past year came to a head. He sat down on the curb, shoulders shaking.

The Shepherd sat down next to him and put a hand on his back. They stayed that way for several minutes.

Finally, The Pastor took a deep breath and got to his feet. His legs were shaking.

"God still has a plan for you," said The Shepherd, who had stood up beside him.

"Yeah, right," muttered The Pastor. For what could there be for him now?

"Look over there," said The Shepherd.

He was pointing to the empty lot where The Church complex had once stood. Homeless men and women and children were huddled around fires in garbage cans, burning hotter than usual on such a cold night. Empty beer cans and gin bottles were scattered everywhere. Piles of blankets and threadbare sleeping bags were gathered as close to the fires as possible. The Pastor shuddered as he thought of what it would be like to sleep outside tonight and he was suddenly glad for his cheap apartment, humble as it was. And he felt a small measure of compassion for these people, in spite of the bad life choices he was sure they'd made.

The Shepherd pointed to the people huddled there. "There is My church," he said.

His voice was exactly the same as the voice the Pastor had heard in his head that night in the hospital. And He was pointing to the same empty lot that had been below the hospital window.

"But there's no church there any more," said The Pastor.

"There is My church," The Shepherd said, again.

The Pastor felt another chill, this time not from the cold. And suddenly it came to him in a rush. This time his vision wasn't of a huge cathedral, nor was it of something that would make him famous.

In that moment he knew what he would do. He'd been given a second calling. Maybe it was the real calling he'd gotten in the first place, the one he'd turned into something for himself.

"Thank you," he said as he turned toward The Shepherd.

But the man was gone.

After a time, The Pastor went forward. He approached a woman who was huddled in front of a garbage can fire, a threadbare blanket wrapped tightly around her. Her world-weary eyes reflected the light of the flames.

"Looks like you could use some company," The Pastor said.

PARABLE 12:
THE VOYAGE

Finally the clouds let go, the rain fell, and the sea swelled. Little Juan raced back and forth on the deck of the boat, laughing, shouting. "Rain, Papa! It's raining!" The boy used the singsong of small children everywhere. "It's raining, it's pouring, the old man is snoring. The old man is singing in his sleep! He's writing a symphony! Si! A symphony!"

"Put on your lifeline, Little Juan," said Papa gently. "Did you already forget what happened the last time it stormed? The sea, she is a fickle woman, and already she is changing. See the waves? In a short while they could cover us with a mountain of water and then where would you be? Down among the sharks."

"But Papa, it has been so long since it has rained. This

is not angry rain. This is gentle rain. Can you smell it? It smells like rich soil, like green beans and apples, like life itself. And it tastes wonderful too, just like lemons with sugar."

"I can see I have been reading to you much too often. My son is becoming a poet. And now . . . lifeline on . . . please."

"Okay, Papa."

He watched Little Juan awkwardly attach the lifeline and felt an old, familiar pride swell his chest like the waves of the sea. The rain did smell fresh and earthy. And it felt like a billion cool caresses on his face when he turned his face upward. And the sound. Ah, the sound was like the soothing rumble of freight trains in the distance on a Castilian summer night. And he might never have noticed, but for Little Juan.

"Shall we stand here now on this bucking deck and watch the storm, my little one?"

"No, Papa. I would rather dance, and try to catch the raindrops with my tongue."

Papa chuckled. "Of course, my son. Of course."

And what had brought them here to this place, this moment? Many things, both happy and sad. A father and a son will travel countless miles together and what makes one moment rise up and say, "Remember this always" is hard to fathom. But for Papa, this was a moment like that.

"Mama says we need to keep sailing east," said Little Juan later, after the rain had passed ahead of them and the sun had reappeared overhead, beating down on their small sailboat and sending up steam from the weathered deck.

Papa did not answer. A few brief images shimmered on the horizon where he looked – images of a woman, her dark hair flowing over copper-colored shoulders, her brown eyes filling with tears of joy as her infant boy drank sweet milk from her breast.

The boat rocked gently. "What shall we do tonight, little one, now that the rain has passed?" asked Papa, changing the subject.

"I would like to go inside the cabin and read some more," answered Little Juan. "I wish the sun would drop into the sea right now, so it would be night."

As if in answer to the boy's words, the sun did indeed sink lower in the sky. It hung on the edge of the horizon behind them for a while, growing larger. At last it flamed out in an explosion of dazzling orange and yellow and purple, and splashed below the rippling line of dark blue water. In this latitude, and so far out at sea, the twilight was short, and soon the sky filled with radiant stars.

Papa checked their bearing one last time and made sure the wheel was fastened securely. The boat glided through the gentle ocean on a steady breeze. There was nothing but open water ahead, but Papa checked anyway.

They stepped inside and Papa lit the hurricane lamp. Shadows swayed and flitted across the wood planking of the tiny cabin as the boat rocked. The odor of aged teakwood filled Papa's nose. It was a smell he had lived with at night for much of his life. A bunk on the high seas had always meant a warm, safe haven to him, and the motion of the waves had rocked him to sleep countless times. They settled in the bunk together and Little Juan snuggled his head against Papa's shoulder.

"What shall we read tonight, little one? Shall it be *Don Quixote*? *Huckleberry Finn*? *The Swiss Family Robinson*?"

"I think I would like *Treasure Island*. We have not read that one as much as the others. I am sure we have only finished it ten or twelve times."

Papa chuckled and reached into a battered footlocker beside the bed. He produced a tattered copy of *Treasure Island* from the precious pile of books inside. He adjusted the hurricane lamp. The pages fell open to the bookmark at chapter thirteen, where they had stopped reading earlier: "We brought up just where the anchor was in the chart, about a third of a mile from either shore, the mainland on one side, and Skeleton Island on the other. The bottom was clean sand. The plunge of our anchor sent up clouds of birds wheeling and crying over the woods. . . ."

As he read the words, troubling thoughts hovered in the back of Papa's mind. He paused and closed his eyes for a moment, trying to make sense of it. They had been lost, drifting on an endless sea, both delirious with fever. How long had it been since then? Ten days? One month? Two months? There seemed to be no passing of time. The sun went down at all different times and the nights seemed to be short and then long and then short again. And neither of them ever slept.

"Papa? You stopped reading," said Little Juan. "Were you dreaming again?"

Papa opened his eyes. "No, my son. I was merely woolgathering. There seems to be a lot of wool inside my head these days. But let us leave that for another day. We have an island of treasure to explore."

The boat rocked gently as Papa read chapter after chapter, until he reached the end, just as sunlight peeked under the bottom of the cabin door: "Oxen and wain-ropes would not bring me back again to that accursed island; and the worst dreams that ever I have are when I hear the surf booming about its coasts or start upright in bed with the sharp voice of Captain Flint still ringing in my ears: 'Pieces of eight! Pieces of eight!'"

This was the happiest time of all, his son safe in his arms and living out a great adventure through the awesome magic of a good story. "That was a fine story, wasn't it?" said Papa, as he stood up and stretched.

"Yes, Papa. What will we read next?"

"You will have to wait until tonight to see. And now, if you wouldn't mind, I would like to spend a few moments alone on the deck. Why don't you stay here awhile and rest your eyes."

"Are you going to think about Mama?"

Papa looked down at his son, reclining on the bunk. He was so young, but he seemed to understand so much. "Yes, I think so," he answered softly.

"Then I will think of her, too," said Little Juan. "She likes it when I think about her."

Papa felt a chill on the back of his neck. Little Juan had been doing that a lot lately, talking as if he could actually hear his mother's voice. But that was impossible.

The salt air filled Papa's nose as he stepped out into the sunlight on the deck. It conjured up images of past voyages, of leaping dolphins and island flowers. The sails fluttered gracefully and the canvas made regular, reassuring flapping noises. The cream color of the sails stood out against the brilliant blue of the sky and the delicate turquoise of the sea. A gentle breeze kept them on a steady course through a rippling sea.

A course to where? wondered Papa, as he gazed toward the east. This was the time of morning, just after sunrise, that his wife had loved the best. Thoughts of her surfaced inside Papa's head, even though he tried to push them back down, to make them disappear. They were thoughts of Sofia, beautiful Sofia, his wife. Wasn't this very boat, *Sofia Marie*, named after her?

Sofia had been a fine woman, an understanding woman. She knew that sailing was in Papa's blood. Ever since he was small, he had dreamed of the sea, of mornings on the ocean just like this. He had worked and studied and apprenticed on countless small ships until he had gained a fine reputation. When the opportunity came to captain a ship across the ocean, he had jumped at the chance. It was what he had worked for, what he had dreamed of. And Sofia had let him go. But it had cost him so much – so very much.

Papa tried to resist the images that seemed to pop up again at the edge of the horizon, to shut his eyes against them, but he could not. They were scenes from his long, ocean voyage, his first after finally becoming captain of his own ship and crew. He saw again the South Sea Islands, like scattered diamonds upon the sea. He saw the exotic ports and harbors where they had stopped. He saw himself standing, aching with loneliness on the deck at night, gazing at the moonlight's rippling path upon the water, leading toward the east and home. He saw his ship cruise into the harbor at the end of the long voyage, home at last. He watched the gangplank drop onto the pier, the quiet, empty pier. There should have been people waiting for them at the harbor – wives, children, old people, but there had been only silence, and a row of fresh graves in the churchyard. Fever, that ancient foe, had unleashed its hot claws upon Papa's village while he had been away.

Papa, lost in his remembrance, didn't notice a dark cloud pass in front of the rising sun, and then another. The wind picked up and the water began to churn, catching the bow of the little boat in crossing waves. Wind tugged on the sails and the boat leaned hard to starboard. A raindrop splashed on the top of Papa's head and coaxed him back to the present. There was more to remember, but for now a storm was gathering. He called to Little Juan and began to trim the sails.

"Papa?" Little Juan had come outside to stand behind his father.

"Yes, little one. Please help me with the sails. It seems that it will rain again, only harder this time."

Little Juan helped Papa with the sails and asked, "Did Mama talk to you?"

"No, my son."

"I heard you talking out here on the deck before I came outside. I thought that you must have been talking to Mama."

"No, I was not talking to Mama." The image of a crude gravestone appeared in Papa's mind – a grim, gray cloud like the ones forming in the sky. He muttered as an after-thought, "Besides, if Mama were here, do you think she would talk to a wretch like me?"

Little Juan looked down at his feet. There had been bitterness in Papa's voice. "Of course Mama would talk to you," he said. "Talking to you is what she wants to do most. She wants to tell you something."

"Your Mama is dead!" said Papa sharply. "Don't you understand? Dead! Now why don't you stop talking like that? There is a storm on the way!"

Lightning flashed overhead and thunder followed - a great, bellowing crash. Little Juan's eyes grew wide and his mouth dropped open, more afraid of the thunder in his father's voice than the rumbling in the sky.

A giant wave swelled up in front of the little boat. Papa grabbed Little Juan with his left arm, as he held onto a swinging boom with his right. The wave crashed over them like surf washing over sand crabs. Papa held on and the boat tipped, nearly capsizing, until it righted itself again. The storm spent its fury in two more towering waves and then was over, as quickly as it had begun.

After the danger had passed off to the east, Little Juan moved away from his father and wiped his face. Water dripped down his nose and onto his trembling lower lip. "I am sorry, Papa," he said. "I did not mean to make you angry." He turned and ran into the cabin.

Papa ran his hand through his thick, black hair. Now what have I done? Maybe I should just leap into the sea and be done with it. The world would be better off. But Papa knew he couldn't do that. He turned toward the cabin and Little Juan.

Papa opened the door and saw his son lying on the bed, his face buried in the pillow, sobbing softly. Papa sat down gently on the bed and tapped his son's shoulder.

"I am very sorry, my little one. I did not mean to scold you."

Little Juan rolled over and looked up into his father's eyes. The tears still came but they were easing now, the last few drops of a rain squall. He reached up his arms and hugged his father's neck.

"There, there," mumbled Papa as he stroked the boy's head. "Can you ever forgive me?"

Little Juan pulled away. "But of course I forgive you. I love you. And when people love you they forgive you no matter what."

Papa had not been expecting a response such as this. It startled him for a moment. Then he took the child fully into his arms and wept.

*****

Papa felt a small hand on his shoulder. He had been lying in his bunk, thinking of Sophia. He sat up and rubbed his eyes. Little Juan was sitting on the edge of the bunk, looking at him with eyes that seemed much older than his years.

"What is it, little one?"

"Are you all right now, Papa?"

Papa hung his head. "I will never be all right."

"Why, Papa?"

Papa glanced around the cabin. The light from outside dimmed. Taps of rain began to fall on the roof. "I must confess something," he said.

"What, Papa?"

Papa paused a moment. How was he to say this? How could he explain it to a nine-year-old?

"Little Juan, I have told you many times how I loved your Mama. Do you know that?"

"Of course, Papa."

"But still, I killed her."

"What do you mean?"

"It is not that I killed her with a knife or a sword. It is not that easy. But I killed her just the same. I should have been there for her, when the fever came. But I was chasing my dreams."

The rain on the cabin roof picked up in intensity and the boat leaned to the side.

Little Juan screwed up his face. "What dreams?" he asked.

"My dreams of sailing the ocean. Since I was smaller than you I have always wanted that. And when I got my chance, I went. And I left you and your mother alone. If I wasn't so selfish I would have stayed home. I could have taken you and her away from the village at the first signs of sickness and she never would have died. Instead I was too late. I took you in this little boat away from the fever, but it was too late for Mama."

Little Juan's eyes brightened. "I'll talk to Mama," he said. "She'll know what to say."

"Your Mama's dead," answered Papa. "She will never

have anything to say, ever again." He turned his head away and began to weep again.

Little Juan stood up and went over by the cabin door. He sat down on the wood floor, hugging his knees, his head cocked to one side. Rain fell softly on the roof of the cabin as Papa wept the night away.

****

"Papa. Papa."

Little Juan shook Papa's shoulder. The first rays of morning sun shone pink through the open cabin door. Papa opened his raw, red eyes. His head ached. All night long he had been thinking of Sophia.

Little Juan put his right hand under Papa's chin and gently lifted his father's head to meet his eyes.

"Mama says you shouldn't be sad," he said.

"Mama's dead," answered Papa.

"Mama wants me to ask you something," continued Little Juan. "Did you know that the fever would come? Before you left on your trip?"

"Of course not."

"If you had known, would you have gone?"

"Of course not, but. . . ."

"So what did you do that was so wrong?" Little Juan looked Papa straight in the eye as he said this, and it seemed that the roles of father and son had been reversed. Papa could think of nothing to say.

"The fever killed Mama," said Little Juan. "Not you. Sometimes people die, even if their whole family is there to hold their hand. Mama wanted you to be a sea captain because it was what you always wanted to be. She wouldn't have let you give up your dreams even if you had tried. She wants you to know that it's all right. You can stop feeling sad now."

Papa shook his head in frustration. "But you can't know a thing like that," he said. "Mama is gone."

Little Juan stood up and took a deep breath. He looked around the room as if he was unsure of what to do next. Finally he spoke. "Take my hand, Papa," he said.

"What?"

"Take my hand."

Papa felt a fluttering in his stomach. Every fiber in his being wanted him to turn away and lie back down. Instead, he stood up and reached out. His fingers quavered as his son's small hand guided him toward the open cabin door.

They walked to the edge of the deck.

"Look there, Papa," said Little Juan.

The sea was like mirrored glass. There was something in the water.

A bank of debris floated slowly on the current and approached the starboard side of their boat. From a distance it looked like simple driftwood, but as it got closer Papa saw that it was wood planking from the wreck of a small boat.

Papa stared. Something about the wreckage was too familiar. It didn't take long for Papa to know why, and it hit him like a knife in his chest.

"See, Papa," said Little Juan.

A piece of weathered, wood planking floated among the

debris. Painted clearly on it were the words *Sofia Marie*.

The suspicion that had been gnawing at the edge of Papa's consciousness for some time now was true after all. The evidence was there in the water, floating in front of his eyes.

"So we died in the storm," he said.

Papa thought of the fever that had come upon them at sea, the confusing days when they both had been delirious, followed by a long gap in his memory. And then they were both on this boat, sailing aimlessly across the water.

"Only one of us died," said Little Juan. "But that doesn't matter now. You just need to know that it's all right. Everything will be all right now."

"One of us?" said Papa, as he struggled to understand. "But. . . ."

"You can let go," said Little Juan. "You don't have to fight any more. Look."

Little Juan pointed to the east. Just at the edge of the horizon was a dark blue smudge, almost like a mirage. Papa's experienced eyes knew what he was looking at.

"Land," he said.

"That's where Mama is," said Little Juan. "She wanted me to sail the last miles with you. And now we're almost there."

****

The Padre caressed the old man's hand. "You can rest now," he said.

He had given the Last Rites when the old man's heart

rate had slowed to almost nothing a few hours ago. But the old man had hung on, breathing once or twice a minute. And then, moments ago, a look of peace had come over the old man's face. He took one last, long breath and then stopped breathing altogether.

The Padre took a sip of water from a glass on the bedside stand. Sometimes life was sad. Forty years ago an English merchant ship had found this man floating on some wreckage at sea, out of his head with exposure. He had no memory of who he was. He spoke Spanish, so they'd brought him to the monastery. He'd been here ever since.

The Padre had tried to help the man remember who he was, but there seemed to be something inside of him, a deep sadness that prevented him from recalling anything before the shipwreck. Only the Lord knew what terrible memories he had been unable to face. The men had become friends over the years, and the Padre had grown very fond of the way the man carried himself, and the grateful way he helped with anything the Padre needed done around the monastery. When the man's heart had become feeble and he'd gone into a coma a month ago, the Padre had nursed him with care, hoping that the man could finally be free from whatever had been tormenting him.

But for the past few days the man had been restless, even within the coma, and it seemed as if he was still fighting the battle. Now the battle was over and he was in God's hands. At least the Padre hoped so.

The Padre pulled the burlap blanket over the man's face. It could have been a trick of the light, but it almost seemed as if the granite-like face was smiling. Was that just wishful thinking? The Padre whispered a short prayer and hoped it was not.

****

Papa looked to the east, a breeze from the south caressing his cheek. The sails filled and the little boat moved smoothly through the water. The sky overhead was full of stars. A soft, yellow moon slowly climbed into the sky ahead of them. At the edge of a rippling path of moonlight the land rose higher out of the water. Flickering lights dotted the shoreline and he could see the outline of a harbor. Little Juan's voice echoed inside his head: "Everything is going to be all right now."

As the shore grew closer, Papa saw a figure there, waving. He recognized the silhouette, for he had dreamed of it often.

"Sophia," he whispered tenderly. He started to call Little Juan to come and see. But suddenly he realized that the boy was no longer on the boat. Instead, he was standing on the shore next to Sofia, waving.

The old man smiled. And then, as the sadness and awful grief dropped away from his heart forever, he trimmed the sails one last time, and, like a feather on the water, his small boat drifted into the harbor.

EPILOGUE:
PEACE OF HEART

We drove through the imposing iron gates of the cemetery on a Sunday summer afternoon. My little girl sat next to me in the middle of the huge front seat, snuggled up against my leg like she always did when we borrowed Grandpa's car. I held her hand as she cuddled her cheek against the shaggy stuffed dog I had just bought her. She had named it "Spots," although there weren't any spots on it; I guess the logic of five-year-olds is sometimes lost on the rest of us.

I had stalled for time by taking her to the toy store to get the puppy. I hadn't really wanted to come here at all. This was my first trip back to the cemetery since I had gotten back into town. All I could think of was that last week at the hospital, the helpless feeling of watching someone die, and the gut-wrenching grief that came later. It was just a lot to face all over again, so I had stalled and stalled. Now, here we were, two years later, my daughter and I going to see Grandma.

My little girl had only been three when her Grandma died. That was one of the things that seemed such a shame, the fact that Mom would never get to see her granddaughter grow up, go to school, get married. I thought of a video I once took of my Mom and my daughter strolling down the sidewalk together. My daughter had been wearing pink, heart-shaped sunglasses that my Mom had just bought for her. Mom's smile lit up that movie. She was so proud to be showing off her first and only granddaughter.

I pulled the big Ford into the parking space in front of the cemetery office. I suppose I should have known where the grave was, but it had been two years. We got out of the car and went inside, my little girl still clinging to her new toy puppy. The cemetery office smelled fresh and nice, not like I had expected. The summer sun shone through cheerful, white curtains. There was a little glass container full of hard candies on the counter.

"Are those free?" my daughter asked tentatively.

A young man behind the desk said, "Help yourself, young lady."

"I'm goin' to see my Grandma," said my daughter. She reached for a piece of candy and unwrapped it methodically while I pored over a map of the gravesites.

A moment later we were back in the car, counting left turns and right turns and forks in the road. I began to recognize things as I tried to ignore the knot in my stomach and the trembling in my throat.

I made a final right turn and eased the car over to the side of the road. "Here we are," I said softly.

A warm, summer breeze blew across my face as I opened the door. I helped my daughter out on my side of the car and I closed the car door behind us. I took a deep breath and grabbed my daughter's hand. No use delaying any longer.

Our tennis shoes made soft, crackling noises as we left the pavement and headed across the August-dry grass. My daughter sensed something in my step and held back a little. She clung to her stuffed dog and looked up at me with blue eyes – her Grandma's eyes.

"It's okay," I said, but my voice sounded weak and far away. "It's just over here."

I remembered the maple tree from the funeral. My Mom was buried at the base of it, next to my Grandpa and Grandma, and across from my brother. There were no tombstones in this quadrant of the cemetery, only brass plates at the head of each grave.

"Look," I said quietly. "There's Grandma." I was seeing the plate for the first time. It seemed so final, her name cast in metal like that. The years were there, too. Born. Died. Just like that.

"Is she under there?" my daughter asked.

"Oh, no, Grandma's in Heaven. They just put her leftover body in the ground so we can come and remember her."

My little girl let go of my hand and bent down to touch the marker. "What's this?" she asked, her hand caressing a musical note, carved underneath my Mom's name on the brass plate.

"That means music. Grandma was very good at music. She played the piano and directed a whole choir of people. In fact, Daddy got his music from Grandma."

"You took her music?"

"Not exactly. Music is something everyone can share, and when you give it to someone, then you both have it. Grandma gave music to a lot of people."

And it was true. When I was young, I used to belittle my Mom's work with the church choir. They had seemed old and off-key to me. But they had all come to the funeral, and had all gone out of their way to tell me how much they were going to miss my Mom. Mom had meant something to all of them, something important. I heard piano music echo inside my head. It was "Silent Night," a song I hadn't been able to listen to since she had died.

"Grandma loved her music," I said, as I knelt down to run my finger over the note on the marker. My throat tightened up and I worried about crying in front of my daughter. "And she gave the music to me. Whenever she came to watch me sing and do my show, and people would laugh and sing along, she would say, 'Music makes people happy.' And she was right about that. And now I play music for my job. All because of your Grandma."

"That sounds nice," said my daughter. "I like it when you sing to me."

"Grandma used to sing to you, too, when you were a baby," I managed to say. "She loved you so very much." In my head, Mom's voice was singing a lullaby. I swallowed hard.

I knelt down and looked at the marker for a minute or so, my little girl caught up in my arms. "Grandma would be very proud of you," I said. "You're getting so big."

My daughter held her puppy up over the marker, as if to show her new toy to Grandma. I eased my daughter down onto the grass and stood up. I looked away, blinking.

So many thoughts rattled around in my head like old bones. Once the grief over Mom's death had subsided, all of us in the family had been hashing things over. Mom should have done this. If only she had done that. How come she had been so organized? Maybe she was too strong-willed. Maybe she should have given us more space. Why couldn't she see things our way? I don't know why, but we all seemed to feel the need to analyze her life, to try and put it into a nice, neat package. But now I had grown tired of analyzing. I didn't want to hear it anymore. I just wanted to remember.

I looked out over the gravestones. There were so many. All those people lying in the ground, all of them born, living out their lives, and now gone. They probably all had families that came out here and hashed things over, and then hashed things over some more after they got home.

I looked into the distance and saw a man standing over a fresh grave. Even from far away I could tell he was hunched over with grief. By another grave a few people stood in a circle and talked in low voices. I wondered what they were talking about. Was it about all the little habits their loved one used to have - things that used to drive everyone crazy? By another grave a woman sat quietly on the ground, not talking, not grieving, just sitting.

I felt most like that woman. I just wanted to think about my Mom, to remember her. The little things we had hashed over so many times had begun to fade, because they were, after all, little things. I thought of the big things, the things we took for granted. Now they were the most important things of all.

"As much as your Grandma loved her music, she loved all of us even more," I said to my daughter as I again pulled her up into my arms. "She would have done anything for us, anything at all. She used to wait for us at the door when we came to visit, and her whole face would light up when we came up the stairs."

I felt a catch in my throat, but it seemed okay. I looked down at my little girl in my arms. "Do you know how I said that because Grandma could play music, that now I can play music too? That she gave music to me, because she loved music . . . but she loved me even more?"

My little girl nodded.

"Well, just like that, because Grandma loved me so much, now I can love you." And I hugged my daughter as hard as I dared.

My daughter smiled then, her blue eyes bright and clear. "I'm glad she loved you so much," she said.

"Me too, Sweetheart," I answered, and decided I was through hashing things out. Through forever.

My daughter pointed across the road at a large, white tombstone. "What does that say?" she asked.

I carried her over to it. "It says Harold Kaputsnik," I answered.

She giggled. "That's a funny name."

She pointed to another stone. "How about this one?"

"Gladys Hornblossom."

"Horn Blossom?" She giggled louder. "That's really silly. How about this one?"

"Gerald Whitehead."

"Did he have a white head?" She laughed so loud that I had to hold her tighter to keep from dropping her. I looked around uneasily, knowing my five-year-old was laughing at the names of deceased people. But there wasn't anyone close by and somehow it seemed okay. And I had started to chuckle a little myself. And I began to look for some names that she would think were funny.

"How about this one?" I asked. "Tom Twiddlebum." The name was actually "Thomas Templeton," but I knew that Twiddlebum was a lot funnier. My daughter thought so too, because she kept on laughing.

For the next ten minutes we wandered around the graveyard, with me "reading" names on headstones, and my little girl laughing hysterically at nearly every name. And pretty soon I was laughing too. For the first time in two years, my heart felt light. It was a classic, late-summer day and everything seemed right with the world. It would have made Mom happy. Maybe it was making her happy.

Finally we tired of the game and I said, "Let's go say good-bye to Grandma, and then we can stop at McDonald's on the way back to Grandpa's house. Your Grandma used to take me there."

We took one more look at my Mom's grave and my daughter held up her puppy one more time for her. I knew then that it had been the right thing to come here, my little girl and I. Even if we never came back, it really didn't matter. Mom wasn't actually here. She was living in my heart, and there was finally peace there.

Again I heard the piano version of "Silent Night" in my head. It was a strange song to be hearing on a warm, August day. But it was one of the songs that made me think of my Mom. And I knew it always would. "Sleep in heavenly peace … sleep in heavenly peace," I whispered, as I gently took my little girl's hand, and turned away from death toward the rest of our lives.

AFTERWORD:

All the stories in this collection are parables, which means they are, by nature, works of fiction. The last story, "Peace of Heart," is something different. This story happened pretty much as I've written it here. I did take my daughter to the cemetery when she was five years old. And it was the first time I went back there myself.

So why did I include the story in this, my first collection of Christian writings? I wanted to pay tribute to my Mom. It was her death to cancer that sent me on a painful journey through depression and grief which ultimately led me to embrace Jesus Christ as my Lord and Savior.

It wasn't anything my Mom said that convinced me, for we had many arguments over the years when my Mom was a believer and I was not. Instead, it was the way she lived her life, and more importantly, the graceful way she dealt with her own death when she knew it was coming.

Before she slipped into a coma she was radiant, because she knew that she was going home to be with Jesus. She would see my brother again, and my grandparents, and all the rest who had gone before.

And the grace she showed at the end of her life was like a beacon to me when I began to ask the big questions during my darkest days.

So I just want to say, "Thanks, Mom." Someday I, too, will travel that same road. And when I do, I can only hope that I will travel it with grace and love, the way you did.

Wayne Faust
Evergreen, Colorado
March 2011

NOTES

NOTES

Resources from Healthy Life Press

New Releases – Fall 2014

Mommy, What's 'Died' Mean? - How the Butterfly Story Helped Little Dave Understand His Grandpa's Death, by Linda Swain Gill; Illustrated by David Lee Bass (a.k.a. "Little Dave") – Designed to assist Christian parents and other adults who love and care about children to talk with them about the difficult subject of death, the story traces a small child's experience following his grandpa's and shows how his mother sensitively answered his questions about death by using simple examples derived from the birth of a butterfly. Little Dave's story is colorfully illustrated and designed for a child and parent or trusted adult to read together. The story has been created especially for children from pre-kindergarten through 4th grade. Discussion questions are included for each story page to help determine how much the child understands. A simple imitation game is also included to help involve the child in the story. Several pages at the end of the book contain suggestions about how to discuss death and dying with children of various ages. (**Full-color printed book:** $14.99; PDF eBook: $9.99; both together: $19.99 – direct from publisher; printed books and eBooks available at *www.Amazon.com*; *www.BN.com*; *www.deepershopping.com*, and wherever books are sold.)

No Worries - Spiritual and Mental Health Counseling for Anxiety, by Elaine Leong Eng, MD – Offering a unique spiritual and mental health perspective on a major malady of our age, this practicing Christian psychiatrist has packed a dose of reality mixed with medicine and faith into a book aimed at informing, inspiring, and equipping those who wish to better help those who struggle with anxiety and related disorders, both inside  and outside the church. As one endorser said, "I travel all over the world. I see fellow believers suffering from different forms of anxiety and worry. Dr. Eng's book gives me tools to recognize when people are suffering and how to encourage them to get the help they need." (Printed book: $19.99; PDF eBook: $9.99; both together: $24.99 – direct from publisher; printed books and eBooks available at *www.Amazon.com*; *www.BN.com*; *www.deepershopping.com*, and wherever books are sold.)

If God Is So Good, Why Do I Hurt So Bad?, by David B. Biebel, DMin – This **25th Anniversary Edition** of a best-selling classic (over 200,000 copies in print worldwide, in a dozen languages) is the book's first major revision since its initial release in 1989. This new version features additional original material related to the conundrum of suffering and faith (with principles learned along the way), and chapter ending questions for personal or group use. Endorser Sheila Walsh wrote, "I believe this is one of the most profound, empathetic and beautiful books ever written on the subject of suffering and loss. There is no attempt to quickly ease our pain but rather, with an understanding born in the crucible God uniquely designed for him, David offers a place to stand, a place to fall and a place to rise again. This book left an indelible mark on my heart over twenty years ago and now with this new release the gift is fresh and fragrant. I highly commend this to you!" (Printed book: $14.99; PDF eBook: $9.99; both together: $19.95 – direct from publisher; printed books and eBooks available at *www.Amazon.com*; *www.BN.com*; *www.deepershopping.com*, and wherever books are sold.)

Earlier Releases

We've Got Mail: The New Testament Letters in Modern English – As Relevant Today as Ever! by Rev. Warren C. Biebel, Jr. – A modern English paraphrase of the New Testament Letters, sure to inspire in readers a loving appreciation for God's Word. (Printed book: $9.95; PDF eBook: $6.95; both together: $15.00 – direct from publisher; printed books and eBooks available at *www.Amazon.com*; *www.BN.com*; *www.deepershopping.com*, and wherever books are sold.)

Hearth & Home – Recipes for Life, by Karey Swan (7th Edition) – Far more than a cookbook, this classic is a life book, with recipes for life as well as for great food. Karey describes how to buy and prepare from scratch a wide variety of tantalizing dishes, while weaving into the book's fabric the wisdom of the ages plus the recipe that she and her husband used to raise their kids. A great gift for Christmas or for a new bride. (Perfect Bound book [8 x 10, glossy cover]: $17.95; PDF eBook: $12.95; both together: $24.95 – direct from publisher; printed books and eBooks available at *www.Amazon.com*; *www.BN.com*; *www.deepershopping.com*, and wherever books are sold.)

Who Me, Pray? Prayer 101: Praying Aloud, for Beginners, by Gary A. Burlingame – Who Me, Pray? is a practical guide for prayer, based on Jesus' direction in "The Lord's Prayer," with examples provided for use in typical situations where you might be asked or expected to pray in public. (Printed book: $6.95; PDF eBook: $2.99; both together: $7.95 – direct from publisher; printed books and eBooks available at *www.Amazon.com*; *www.BN.com*; *www.deepershopping.com*, and wherever books are sold.)

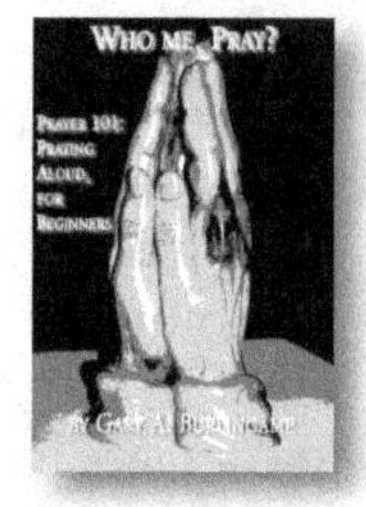

My Broken Heart Sings, the poetry of Gary Burlingame – In 1987, Gary and his wife Debbie lost their son Christopher John, at only six months of age, to a chronic lung disease. This life-changing experience gave them a special heart for helping others through similar loss and pain. (Printed book: $10.95; PDF eBook: $6.95; both together: $13.95 – direct from publisher; printed books and eBooks available at *www.Amazon.com*; *www. BN.com*; *www.deepershopping.com*, and wherever books are sold.)

After Normal: One Teen's Journey Following Her Brother's Death, by Diane Aggen – Based on a journal the author kept following her younger brother's death. It offers helpful insights and understanding for teens facing a similar loss or for those who might wish to understand and help teens facing a similar loss. (Printed book: $11.95; PDF eBook: $6.95; both together: $15.00 – direct from publisher; printed books and eBooks

available at *www.Amazon.com*; *www.BN.com*; *www.deepershopping.com*, and wherever books are sold.)

In the Unlikely Event of a Water Landing – Lessons Learned from Landing in the Hudson River, by Andrew Jamison, MD – The author was flying standby on US Airways Flight 1549 toward Charlotte on January 15, 2009, from New York City, where he had been interviewing for a residency position. Little did he know that the next stop would be the Hudson River. Riveting and inspirational, this book would be especially helpful for people in need of hope and encouragement. (Printed book: $8.95; PDF eBook: $6.95; both together: $12.95 – direct from publisher; printed books and eBooks available at *www.Amazon.com*; *www.BN.com*; *www.deepershopping.com*, and wherever books are sold.)

Finding Martians in the Dark – Everything I Needed to Know About Teaching Took Me Only 30 Years to Learn, by Dan M. Biebel – Packed with wise advice based on hard experience, and laced with humor, this book is a perfect teacher's gift year-round. Susan J. Wegmann, PhD, says, "Biebel's sardonic wit is mellowed by a genuine love for kids and teaching. . . . A Whitman-like sensibility flows through his stories of teaching, learning, and life."

(Printed book: $10.95; PDF eBook: $6.95; Together: $15.00 – direct from publisher; printed books and eBooks available at *www.Amazon.com*; *www.BN.com*; *www.deepershopping.com*, and wherever books are sold.)

Because We're Family and **Because We're Friends**, by Gary A. Burlingame – Sometimes things related to faith can be hard to discuss with your family and friends. These booklets are designed to be given as gifts, to help you open the door to discussing spiritual matters with family members and friends who are open to such a conversation. (Printed book: $5.95 each; PDF eBook: $4.95 each; both together: $9.95 [printed & eBook of the same title] – direct from publisher; printed books and eBooks available at *www.Amazon.com*; *www.BN.com*; *www.deepershopping.com*, and wherever books are sold.)

The Transforming Power of Story: How Telling Your Story Brings Hope to Others and Healing to Yourself, by Elaine Leong Eng, MD, and David B. Biebel, DMin – This book demonstrates, through multiple true life stories, how sharing one's story, especially in a group setting, can bring hope to listeners and healing to the one who shares. Individuals facing difficulties will find this book greatly encouraging. (Printed book: $14.99; PDF eBook: $9.99; both together: $19.99 – direct from publisher; printed books and eBooks available at *www.Amazon.com*; *www.BN.com*; *www.deepershopping.com*, and wherever books are sold.)

You Deserved a Better Father: Good Parenting Takes a Plan, by Robb Brandt, MD – About parenting by intention, and other lessons the author learned through the loss of his firstborn son. It is especially for parents who believe that bits and pieces of leftover time will be enough for their own children. (Printed book: $12.95 each; PDF eBook: $6.95; both together: $17.95 – direct from publisher; printed books and eBooks available at *www.Amazon.com*; *www.BN.com*; *www.deepershopping.com*, and wherever books are sold.)

eBook Cover

Printed Cover

Jonathan, You Left Too Soon, by David B. Biebel, DMin – One pastor's journey through the loss of his son, into the darkness of depression, and back into the light of joy again, emerging with a renewed sense of mission. (Printed book: $12.95; PDF eBook: $5.99; both together: $15.00 – direct from publisher; printed books and eBooks available at *www.Amazon.com*; *www.BN.com*; *www.deepershopping. com*, and wherever books are sold.)

Unless otherwise noted on the site itself, shipping is free for all products purchased through www.healthylifepress.com.

The Spiritual Fitness Checkup for the 50-Something Woman, by Sharon V. King, PhD – Following the stages of a routine medical exam, the author describes ten spiritual fitness "checkups" midlife women can conduct to assess their spiritual health and tone up their relationship with God. Each checkup consists of the author's personal reflections, a Scripture reference for meditation, and a "Spiritual Pulse Check," with exercises readers can use for personal application. (Printed book: $8.95; PDF eBook: $6.95; both together: $12.95 – direct from publisher; printed books and eBooks available at *www.Amazon.com*; *www.BN.com*; *www.deepershopping.com*, and wherever books are sold.)

The Other Side of Life – Over 60? God Still Has a Plan for You, by Rev. Warren C. Biebel, Jr. – Drawing on biblical examples and his 60-plus years of pastoral experience, Rev. Biebel helps older (and younger) adults understand God's view of aging and the rich life available to everyone who seeks a deeper relationship with God as they age. Rev. Biebel explains how to: Identify God's ongoing plan for your life; Rely on faith to manage the anxieties of aging;  Form positive, supportive relationships; Cultivate patience; Cope with new technologies; Develop spiritual integrity; Understand the effects of dementia; Develop a Christ-centered perspective of aging. (Printed book: $10.95; PDF eBook: $6.95; both together: $15.00 – direct from publisher; printed books and eBooks available at *www.Amazon.com*; *www.BN.com*; *www.deepershopping.com*, and wherever books are sold.)

My Faith, My Poetry, by Gary A. Burlingame – This unique book of Christian poetry is actually two in one. The first collection of poems, A Day in the Life, explores a working parent's daily journey of faith. The reader is carried from morning to bedtime, from "In the Details," to "I Forgot to Pray," back to "Home Base," and finally to "Eternal Love Divine." The second collection of poems, Come Running, is wonder, joy, and faith wrapped up in words that encourage and inspire the mind and the heart. (Printed book: $10.95; PDF eBook: $6.95; both together: $13.95 – direct from publisher; printed books and eBooks available at *www.Amazon.com*; *www.BN.com*; *www.deepershopping.com*, and wherever books are sold.)

On Eagles' Wings, by Sara Eggleston – One woman's life journey from idyllic through chaotic to joy, carried all the way by the One who has promised to never leave us nor forsake us. Remarkable, poignant, moving, and inspiring, this autobiographical account will help many who are facing difficulties that seem too great to overcome or even bear at all. It is proof that Isaiah 40:31 is as true today as when it was penned, "But they that wait upon the LORD shall renew their strength; they shall mount up with wings as eagles; they shall run, and not be weary; and they shall walk, and not faint." (Printed book: $14.95; PDF eBook: $8.95; both together: $22.95 – direct from publisher; printed books and eBooks available at *www.Amazon.com*; *www.BN.com*; *www.deepershopping.com*, and wherever books are sold.)

Richer Descriptions, by Gary A. Burlingame – A unique and handy manual, covering all nine human senses in seven chapters, for Christian speakers and writers. Exercises and a speaker's checklist equip speakers to engage their audiences in a richer experience. Writing examples and a writer's guide help writers bring more life to the characters and scenes of their stories. Bible references encourage a deeper appreciation of being created by God for a sensory existence. (Printed book: $15.95; PDF eBook: $8.95; both together: $22.95 – direct from publisher; printed books and eBooks available at *www.Amazon.com*; *www.BN.com*; *www.deepershopping.com*, and wherever books are sold.)

Treasuring Grace, by Rob Plumley and Tracy Roberts – This novel was inspired by a dream. Liz Swanson's life isn't quite what she'd imagined, but she considers herself lucky. She has a good husband, beautiful children, and fulfillment outside of her home through volunteer work. On some days she doesn't even notice the dull ache in her heart. While she's preparing for their summer kickoff at Lake George, the ache disappears and her sudden happiness is mistaken for anticipation of their weekend. However, as the family heads north, there are clouds on the horizon that have nothing to do with the weather. Only Liz's daughter, who's found some of her mother's hidden journals, has any idea what's wrong. But by the end of the weekend, there will be no escaping the truth or its painful buried secrets.

(Printed: $12.95; PDF eBook: $7.95; both together: $19.95 – direct from publisher; printed books and eBooks available at *www.Amazon.com*; *www.BN.com*; *www.deepershopping.com*, and wherever books are sold.)

From Orphan to Physician – The Winding Path, by Chun-Wai Chan, MD – From the foreword: "In this book, Dr. Chan describes how his family escaped to Hong Kong, how they survived in utter poverty, and how he went from being an orphan to graduating from Harvard Medical School and becoming a cardiologist. The writing is fluent, easy to read and understand. The sequence of events is realistic, emotionally moving, spiritually touching, heartwarming, and thought provoking. The book illustrates . . . how one must have faith in order to walk through life's winding path." (Printed book: $14.95; PDF eBook: $8.95; both together: $22.95 – direct from publisher; printed books and eBooks available at *www.Amazon.com*; *www.BN.com*; *www.deepershopping.com*, and wherever books are sold.)

12 Parables, by Wayne Faust – Timeless Christian stories about doubt, fear, change, grief, and more. Using tight, entertaining prose, professional musician and comedy performer Wayne Faust manages to deal with difficult concepts in a simple, straightforward way. These are stories you can read aloud over and over—to your spouse, your family, or in a group setting. Packed with emotion and just enough mystery to keep you wondering, while

providing lots of points to ponder and discuss when you're through, these stories relate the gospel in the tradition of the greatest speaker of parables the world has ever known, who appears in them often. (Printed book: $14.95; PDF eBook: $8.95; both together: $22.95 – direct from publisher; printed books and eBooks available at *www.Amazon.com*; *www.BN.com*; *www.deepershopping.com*, and wherever books are sold.)

The Answer is Always "Jesus," by Aram Haroutunian, who gave children's sermons for 15 years at a large church in Golden, Colorado—well over 500 in all. This book contains 74 of his most unforgettable presentations—due to the children's responses. Pastors, homeschoolers, parents who often lead family devotions, or other storytellers will find these stories, along with comments about props and how to prepare and present them, an invaluable asset in reconnecting with the simplest, most profound truths of Scripture, and then to envision how best to communicate these so even a child can understand them. (Printed book: $12.95; PDF eBook: $8.95; both together: $19.95 – direct from publisher; printed books and eBooks available at *www.Amazon.com*; *www.BN.com*; *www.deepershopping.com*, and wherever books are sold.)

Handbook of Faith, by Rev. Warren C. Biebel, Jr. – The New York Times World 2011 Almanac claimed that there are 2 billion, 200 thousand Christians in the world, with "Christians" being defined as "followers of Christ." The original 12 followers of Christ changed the world; indeed, they changed the history of the world. So this author, a pastor with over 60 years' experience, poses and answers this logical question: "If there are so many 'Christians' on this planet, why are they so relatively ineffective in serving the One they claim to follow?" Answer: Because, unlike Him, they do not know and trust the Scriptures, implicitly. This little volume will help you do that. (Printed book: $8.95; PDF eBook: $6.95; both together: $13.95 – direct from publisher; printed books and eBooks available at *www.Amazon.com*; *www.BN.com*; *www.deepershopping.com*, and wherever books are sold.)

Pieces of My Heart, by David L. Wood – Eighty-two lessons from normal everyday life. David's hope is that these stories will spark thoughts about God's constant involvement and intervention in our lives and stir a sense of how much He cares about every detail that is important to us. The piece missing represents his son, Daniel, who died in a fire shortly before his first birthday. (Printed book: $16.95; PDF eBook: $8.95; both together: $24.95 – direct from publisher; printed books and eBooks available at *www.Amazon.com*; *www.BN.com*; *www.deepershopping.com*, and wherever books are sold.)

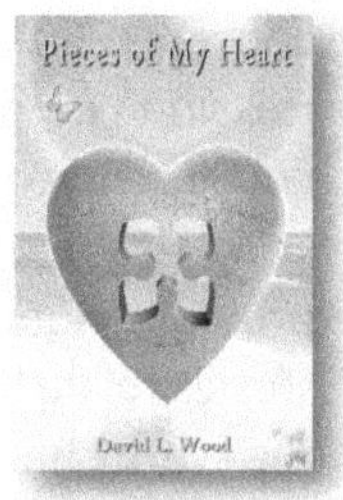

Unless otherwise noted on the site itself, shipping is free for all products purchased through www.healthylifepress.com.

Dream House, by Justa Carpenter – Written by a New England builder of several hundred homes, the idea for this book came to him one day as he was driving that came to him one day as was driving from one job site to another. He pulled over and recorded it so he would remember it, and now you will remember it, too, if you believe, as he does, that "... He who has begun a good work in you will complete it until the day of Jesus Christ." (Printed book: $10.95; PDF eBook: $6.95; both together: $13.95 – direct from publisher; printed books and eBooks available at *www.Amazon.com*; *www.BN.com*; *www.deepershopping.com*, and wherever books are sold.)

A Simply Homemade Clean, by homesteader Lisa Barthuly – "Somewhere along the path, it seems we've lost our gumption, the desire to make things ourselves," says the author. "Gone are the days of 'do it yourself.' Really ... why bother? There are a slew of retailers just waiting for us with anything and everything we could need; packaged up all pretty, with no thought or effort required. It is the manifestation of 'progress' ... right?" I don't buy

that!" Instead, Lisa describes how to make safe and effective cleansers for home, laundry, and body right in your own home. This saves money and avoids exposure to harmful chemicals often found in commercially produced cleansers. (**Full-color** printed book: $16.99; PDF eBook: $6.95; both together: $22.95 – direct from publisher; printed books and eBooks available at *www.Amazon.com*; *www.BN.com*; *www.deepershopping.com*, and wherever books are sold.)

The Secret of Singing Springs, by Monte Swan – One Colorado family's treasure-hunting adventure along the trail of Jesse James. The Secret of Singing Springs is written to capture for children and their parents the spirit of the hunt—the hunt for treasure as in God's Truth, which is the objective of walking the Way of Wisdom that is described in Proverbs. (Printed book: $12.95, PDF eBook: $9.99; both together: $19.99 – direct from publisher; printed books and eBooks available at *www.Amazon.com*; *www.BN.com*; *www.deepershopping.com*, and wherever books are sold.)

God Loves You Circle, by Michelle Johnson – Daily inspiration for your deeper walk with Christ. This collection of short stories of Christian living will make you laugh, make you cry, but most of all make you contemplate—the meaning and value of walking with the Master moment-by-moment, day-by-day. (**Full-color** printed book: $17.95; PDF eBook: $9.99; both together: $22.99 – direct from publisher; printed books and eBooks available at *www.Amazon.com*; *www.BN.com*; *www.deepershopping.com*, and wherever books are sold.)

Our God-Given Senses, by Gary A. Burlingame – Did you know humans have NINE senses? The Bible draws on these senses to reveal spiritual truth. We are to taste and see that the Lord is a good. We are to carry the fragrance of Christ. Our faith is produced upon hearing. Jesus asked Thomas to touch him. God created us for a sensory experience and that is what you will find in this book. (Printed book: $12.99; PDF eBook: $9.99; both together: $19.99 – direct from publisher; printed books and eBooks available at *www.Amazon.com*; *www.BN.com*; *www.deepershopping.com*, and wherever books are sold.)

Vows, a Romantic novel by F. F. Whitestone – When the police cruiser pulled up to the curb outside, Faith Framingham's heart skipped a beat, for she could see that Chuck, who should have been driving, was not in the vehicle. Chuck's partner, Sandy, stepped out slowly. Sandy's pursed lips and ashen face spoke volumes. Faith waited by the front door, her hands clasped tightly, to counter the fact that her mind was already reeling. "Love never fails." A compelling story. (Printed book: $12.99; PDF eBook: $9.99; both together, $19.99 – direct from publisher; printed books and eBooks available at *www.Amazon.com*; *www.BN.com*; *www.deepershopping.com*, and wherever books are sold.)

Unless otherwise noted on the site itself, shipping is free for all products purchased through <u>www.healthylifepress.com</u>.

Worth the Cost?, by Jack Tsai, MD – The author was happily on his way to obtaining the American Dream until he decided to take seriously Jesus' command, "Come, follow me." Join him as he explores the cost of medical education and Christian discipleship. Planning to serve God in your future vocation? Take care that your desires do not get side-tracked by the false promises of this world. What you should be doing now so when you are done with your training you will still want to serve God. (Printed book: $12.99, PDF eBook: $9.99; both together: $19.99 – direct from publisher; printed books and eBooks available at *www.Amazon.com*; *www.BN.com*; *www.deepershopping.com*, and wherever books are sold.)

Nature: God's Second Book – An Essential Link to Restoring Your Personal Health and Wellness: Body, Mind, and Spirit, by Elvy P. Rolle – An inspirational book that looks at nature across the seasons of nature and of life. It uses the biblical Emmaus Journey as an analogy for life's journey, and offers ideas for using nature appreciation and exploration to reduce life's stresses. The author shares her personal story of how she came to grips with this concept after three trips to the emergency room. (**Full-color** printed book: $12.99; PDF eBook $8.99; both together: $16.99 – direct from publisher; printed books and eBooks available at *www.Amazon.com*; *www.BN.com*; *www.deepershopping.com*, and wherever books are sold.)

He Waited, by LaDonna Cooper – Inspires readers to wait upon the Lord for His best for them; stresses the importance of putting God's purpose above one's own; emphasizes that God's love is unconditional; demonstrates the wisdom of waiting, through a combination of positive insights, encouragement, biblical examples and principles. Decorated with original poetry by the author. For singles and others who are waiting. Distributed primarily through *www.Amazon.com*. (Printed book: $10.99; PDF eBook: $9.99; both together: $15.99 – direct from publisher; printed books and eBooks available at *www.Amazon.com*; *www.BN.com*; *www.deepershopping.com*, and wherever books are sold.)

The Big Black Book – What the Christmas Tree Saw, by Rev. Warren C. Biebel, Jr. – An original Christmas story, from the perspective of the Christmas tree. This little book is especially suitable for parents to read to their children at Christmas time or all year-round. (**Full-color** printed book: $9.95; PDF eBook: $4.95; both together: $12.95 – direct from publisher; printed books and eBooks available at *www.Amazon.com*; *www.BN.com*; *www.deepershopping.com*, and wherever books are sold.)

ABOUT HEALTHY LIFE PRESS

Healthy Life Press was founded with a primary goal of helping previously unpublished authors to get their works to market, and to reissue worthy, previously published works that were no longer available. Our mission is to help people toward optimal vitality by providing resources promoting physical, emotional, spiritual, and relational health as viewed from a Christian perspective. We see health as a verb, and achieving optimal health as a process—a crucial process for followers of Christ if we are to love the Lord with all our heart, soul, mind, AND strength, and our neighbors as ourselves—for as long as He leaves us here. We are a collaborative and cooperative small Christian publisher. We share costs/we share proceeds.

For information about publishing with us, e-mail: healthylifepress@aol.com.